LATE PAYMENTS

ALSO BY MICHAEL Z. LEWIN

LATE PAY-MENTS

MICHAEL
Z. LEWIN

WILLIAM
MORROW AND
COMPANY, INC.
NEW YORK

Library of Congress Cataloging-in-Publication Data

Lewin, Michael Z.
  Late payments.

  I. Title.
PS3562.E929L3   1986   813'.54   85-25927
ISBN 0-688-04342-9

Printed in the United States of America

First Edition

1 2 3 4 5 6 7 8 9 10

BOOK DESIGN BY JAYE ZIMET

TO JULIE, AND TO JOHN AND MARY

LATE PAYMENTS

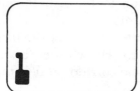 As Powder approached along the corridor, two men, handcuffed together, passed through the door of the Homicide and Robbery with Violence reception area. The men negotiated the passage easily, as if experienced in handcuff navigation. The taller man was in his early forties, well groomed and well dressed. He wore wide-eyed metal-framed glasses and stepped lightly. The shorter man was fat and forty-five, with stubble on his chins. He moved heavily inside a rumpled suit.

It was the shorter man who was the policeman. He nodded to Powder as they approached.

Powder said, "Edwards," as acknowledgment.

As they passed close, the prisoner man suddenly pulled Detective Edwards to a stop and pointed at Powder with his free hand.

"Hey, I know that guy. I know him. I know you, buddy. Your name is Powder, isn't it?"

Powder stopped and pivoted to face the two men.

"You're the cop that sent his son to jail, aren't you? You're Ricky Powder's dad. Hey, ain't that something! Rick and me shared a cell and we used to have spitting contests at a picture of you."

Edwards jerked at his prisoner. "Come on, Morgan." But Morgan maintained his eye contact with Powder.

Powder said, "I'm Ricky Powder's father. And I'd like to put a question to you, something for you to ponder on. The question is this: If the son of a cop can go down for eighteen months, just what do you think is in store for a return visitor like you, Mr. Morgan?"

Powder turned abruptly and strode away from Edwards and his prisoner.

By the time he had walked through the Detective Day Room to his mail slot Powder was chuckling to himself. In one sense he enjoyed his limited kind of fame.

He was pleasantly surprised to find the copies of the new salary schedules he had been promised. He whistled as he walked back, past the desks, through the corridor and to the stairs.

The Indianapolis Police Department stairwells require a key to enter and to leave—to reduce their potential for assisting premature departures from police custody. But needing keys also makes it harder for policemen to use the stairs as an exercise supplement. Only the more determined officers use them regularly.

After descending three flights, Powder emerged on the first floor, the public access level of the half of the City-County Building occupied by the Indianapolis Police Department.

He turned left and immediately collided with a thin, fresh-faced boy with dark hair sticking out on both sides under an Indianapolis Indians baseball cap. The boy looked about twelve.

"Hey!" the boy said.

"Sorry," Powder said.

"Are you a cop?"

Powder looked down at him. He said, "Yes."

"Hey, where do I go to tell somebody my dad is gone?"

"Gone? You mean dead?"

"Who says he's dead?"

"You mean missing? Your father is missing?"

"Yeah," the boy said suspiciously, his narrowed eyes pulling his face into a frown.

"The Missing Persons office is there," Powder said. He pointed down the hall. "But—"

"That place is closed," the boy interrupted. "It says on the door. So where do I go instead?"

"Did somebody point me out to you?"

The boy shook his head.

"I was just the first person to come along?"

"After I saw that office was closed, yeah."

"Well, son, let's go open the office again, shall we?"

Powder led the way to a door that read MISSING PERSONS. A roller blind behind the glass gave a list of opening hours. Powder unlocked the door and they went in.

His kingdom. He had been more than five years in charge of the section and had bullied and connived and publicized and made it grow to include three full-time officers besides himself. Also a civilian who dealt with computer and clerical records.

"My desk is back here," Powder said, and raising the counter flap, he pointed to where he wanted the boy to go.

When they were settled, Powder said, "OK. Your father is gone. Tell me about it."

"I got home from practice and he wasn't there."

"He's usually there?"

"No, but when he ain't he leaves a note. He *always* leaves a note. Every single time."

Powder stared at the boy.

"Today there wasn't no note."

Before Powder locked up again, he wrote *Be worth it* on the new salary schedule. He put the copies on the appropriate desks.

He stood at the door and looked over the room. During his reign Missing Persons had become a more fashionable section, and one of the most effective in the whole Department. He could prove it. He had proved it publicly and privately many times.

Powder felt profoundly dissatisfied.

He locked the door.

■ ■ ■

After parking on the street in front of his house, Powder walked the path and then the ramp up to his front door. He lived on the bottom floor in an ornate nineteenth-century building in an ornate nineteenth-century part of Indianapolis. It was close to the city center, but there was no longer any pressure for redevelopment because of recognition of its "heritage." In recent years the fashion had been for "rehabilitation" instead and a lot of rotten wood had been replaced. At the same time, and at the same pace, a lot of longtime resident families had been replaced by households containing college degrees. The net effect was to make the area, Lockerbie, a desirable one.

Powder, a new boy less than ten years before, was now a comparative old-timer and in the right company he could cluck about the newcomers with the best of them.

In his letter box Powder found a leaflet from the Campaign Against the River Project. CARP. The name rolled nimbly off the tongue. He carried the leaflet to his kitchen and put it on the table.

In the kitchen he hung his jacket on a hook and put on an apron. For half an hour he dusted and vacuumed. Then he took a shower. He dried and talced and combed and dressed in clean clothes.

He went back to the kitchen and picked up the CARP leaflet and carried it to the living room. He read about the millions to be spent developing the White River area and the millions already spent on capital projects to make Indianapolis "great." He had begun to read about the lack of spending on the Indianapolis poor when the doorbell rang.

He put the leaflet down and answered the bell promptly.

On the step was a woman in her early thirties with long black hair. "Long time no see," she said.

"You're late," Powder said.

"Like hell. Out of the way."

Powder stepped back and the woman, Carollee Fleetwood, rolled her wheelchair across the threshold.

"Did you know that there had been no increase in real
spending on literacy or self-help projects for the poor in this
city in the last ten years?"

"No," she said.

"Did you know—"

"Lieutenant, are you going to stand there and talk all
night?"

"Probably," Powder said. He rubbed his face with both
hands. Then he stepped behind her chair, took the handles
and pushed her into the room next to the living room, his
guest bedroom.

"Sergeant, this is a damned uncharitable city when it
comes to its poor and its halt and its lame."

He lifted her gently from her chair and sat her on the edge
of the bed.

She smiled and said, "Do you remember the first time you
shifted me out of that thing?"

"Yeah," he said.

"You poured with sweat."

"I figured if I dropped you, you'd break into pieces."

"It was funny and sweet."

"Not quite the way I remember it," he said.

She took one of his hands. "Make me forget a bit now."

After a drive across the city from Fleetwood's house, they
pulled into a parking lot that was in the center of a horseshoe
of single-story apartments specially designed for disabled
tenants.

Powder unpacked Fleetwood's wheelchair and helped her
into it. "Where we going?" he asked.

"Nine. It's down the side, over there."

Powder guided her to the designated door. Fleetwood
pushed the bell, which was at a level easily accessible to people in wheelchairs.

The door flew open and a tanned man in his late twenties greeted them exuberantly. "Carollee, honey! Hello! Hey, lay some rubber on me!"

Fleetwood rolled herself across the sill-less doorway and bumped a tire of her chair into a tire of the man's wheelchair.

Then the man withdrew, saying, "And this is your supercop boss. Come in, come in, Lieutenant Powder. You look funny without a wheelchair, but we try to be tolerant of weirdos around here. I'm Jules Mencelli, but most people call me Ace."

Powder stepped forward and the men shook hands. "Pleased to meet you, Ace."

"Me too, me too," Mencelli bubbled. He rolled farther back into the room where a table was set with three places. "I feel better already. Hey, you guys like curry? Like nice, hot, India Indian-style curry?"

"Never tried it," Powder said.

"Well then, let's eat first," Mencelli said. "And if you survive it, then I'll tell you why I think somebody's trying to kill me."

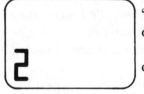

"Where the hell is everybody?" Powder asked, loud, irritated.

"Attending anticompulsiveness classes," Fleetwood said.

"Oh, great."

"We don't open for half an hour, Powder. What the hell do you expect?"

"I expect? Nothing is what I expect. What I want—that's different."

"They're young. They look at you. They don't want to end up like you. So they act differently from you."

Powder suddenly smiled and nodded. "Reasonable. No sane person would want to end up in charge of a bunch of cripples and whiners and children."

Fifteen minutes later, as they both were dealing with paper work, Powder suddenly said, "Suppose you are the father of a twelve-year-old son."

"What?"

"I said—"

"I heard what you said."

"OK. A year and a half ago your wife ran off with another guy, leaving you and the kid flat. It shook you up, but you've really made an effort with him and the two of you are getting along fine. The kid's doing all right in school and this year he's going out for the freshman baseball team."

Fleetwood frowned. "I thought you said he was twelve."

"I did."

"He's at high school?"

"His birthday's soon."

"All right," Fleetwood said. Then, "How do I make my living?"

"Factory work, but it varies a bit, so sometimes you're home when the kid is home and sometimes you're not. But the one thing you always do, never fail, is leave a note for the kid when you aren't going to be there when he gets back from school."

"How often is that?"

"Could be three, four times a week."

"And?"

"Yesterday you weren't there and you didn't leave the kid a note."

"Why not?"

"That's what I want you to tell me!" Powder boomed.

"Why didn't you leave the kid a note, eh? Why yesterday?"

From behind them a cheerful voice said, "Hello, hello! Where is everybody this morning?"

Powder turned fiercely to Sue Swatts, one of the two junior officers assigned to Missing Persons, and said, "I want to know that too."

"What did I do?" Swatts asked Fleetwood.

By ten o'clock two men were waiting in the office for their turn with the other junior officer, Howard Haddix, who was working "in" for the day.

Sue Swatts asked Powder whether she should help out at the counter. It would mean a delay in preparing the "Have You Seen Them?" leaflet that was Swatt's major task each week. The office now distributed more than six hundred to places where "missing" people might be seen, if the right person was paying the right attention. One of Powder's main strategies was to try to harness eyes in key places throughout the county.

Powder studied the waiting men. "No," he said. "They don't look agitated enough."

Perfectly satisfied with the response, Swatts returned to her work.

At eleven Powder left the office and climbed the stairs to the Computer Records Room on the fourth floor. He passed by a glass-paneled Inquiry bay in the hall and entered the large, open room. He tapped the desk of the nearest officer, who was staring into a visual display terminal with no apparent zeal. "I want to see Lieutenant Tidmarsh. He around?"

The officer nodded without changing the direction of his glaze.

Tidmarsh's door was partly open and when he approached, Powder could see the acting head of the newly expanded computer section concentrating on another VDT. Powder knocked on the door and walked in and sat down. "First rest I've had all day," he said.

Tidmarsh did not look at him.

"You know," Powder said, "the know-it-all brass really get up my nose when they knock me for publicizing the successes we have down in Missing Persons."

"Hello, Powder," Tidmarsh said without looking up.

"They complain because whenever we get a splash in the papers, we get another stack of new cases. Now I just can't see complaining about that. It's like complaining about finding a hundred new people with cancer. The cases are there even if we didn't budget for them. Our real problem is *getting* the public to come to us, *getting* them to think we can help. Once we know the real size of the missing persons problem, we can reallocate the appropriate resources to deal with it, and give a better service."

Tidmarsh turned to Powder at last and leaned back in his chair. "I can remember the days when you eschewed publicity, Leroy. In fact, you were the bane of the Press Department because you wouldn't let reporters and photographers in your precious department."

"Ah," Powder said, holding up a hand to forestall more comments in the same vein. "That wasn't the right kind of publicity."

Tidmarsh scoffed mildly. "Keeping busy?" he asked ingenuously.

"They're stacked up three-deep down there, they really are," Powder said.

"What can I do for you?"

"I want any arrest and conviction records on one Sidney Arthur Sweet."

Tidmarsh blinked.

"That's not a problem, is it?"

Tidmarsh put his hands flat together. "No. But you do have a computer terminal downstairs you can use for that kind of thing."

"Oh, I know," Powder said. "But my new operator—have

you met him? A kid called Noble Perkins. Sounds like he's fresh from the cornfields, but a wizard on his machines. Young Noble is so busy down there, smoke is almost coming off the keyboard. So I thought I'd save him the bother and come up myself."

"That's very decent of you," Tidmarsh said. "That's one thing they say about you, Powder. You look after your people."

"I think of my role as like that of a basketball coach."

"You do?"

"My job is to give the members of my team the best possible chance to do their jobs."

"Speaking of your team, how is the gorgeous Sergeant Fleetwood these days?"

"Still can't walk," Powder said, shaking his head. "They promised me she'd be sprinting in six months when they sent her along, but it was all bull." Powder shrugged exaggeratedly to show his resignation.

"Come off it, Powder! A genuine heroine, refuses to retire, comes back into service and finds lost kids. Photogenic with it. She's a gold mine for you. And you know it; I read the papers."

"She can do a few things despite her immobility," Powder conceded. "I don't exactly get the cream of the crop in this place. So I have to make do."

Tidmarsh sat in silence a moment.

"Hey," Powder said, "congratulations on your promotion."

"It's only 'acting,'" Tidmarsh said. "But thanks."

"You'll get confirmed, no problem. You're good. I always said you were good. I recognize quality, even if I don't get much of it to work with. Everyone I see is either Hopalong Cassidy on crutches or they got wheat kernels in their hair."

Tidmarsh repeated his silence. Then he said, "I have the feeling that you are leading someplace, Powder. But I can't for the life of me see where."

"Well," Powder said, "funny you should say. But I got this hypothetical question been preying on my mind, and yes, I'd like your professional advice. As the head of the most sophisticated computer section we've ever had here."

"Acting head," Tidmarsh said, without being able to help himself.

"You'll get confirmed," Powder said again. "Everybody knows that."

"What's the question?"

"Strictly hypothetical," Powder said.

"Yeah."

"Well, let's suppose that *I* am a computer guy."

Tidmarsh raised his eyebrows.

"Now I cover the whole damn state of Indiana. I run—actually I work for the guy who runs—the state's biggest central statistical computer service."

"Part of the census department?"

"Yeah, sort of," Powder said enthusiastically. "It's a special big project based on that. So I have access, in principle, to all the personal data about people that Indiana has on formal records. And in practice, I can get into a lot of the other information banks around the state. Health stuff, spinoffs from the government census, credit ratings . . . all kinds of thing."

Tidmarsh nodded slowly.

"Now, I just happen to have had a motorcycle accident when I was seventeen and I lost both my legs in it. And I also just happen to have some spare time at work."

"OK."

"So, instead of using my idle hours to go to roller discos, I work up a program which goes through the state records and calculates the life expectancy of people of my age, which is twenty-nine, who happen not to have any legs. Actually what I work on is people who have 'mobility disablement,' since 'no legs' isn't one of the standard medical categories."

Tidmarsh lifted his eyes and the lids fluttered for a moment. "All right," he said. "An actuarial calculation. If you have the data . . . OK."

"Data seems to be my middle name," Powder said.

"And what do you find?"

"I get a result."

"So what is the question?"

"Hang on," Powder snapped. "So I get a number, right?"

"Right."

"Now what the number shows is that I am likely to die earlier than guys not in wheelchairs, but there is a certain logic to that because some of the guys in wheelchairs aren't very well guys. Not like me, who is bursting with pus and vinegar."

"OK."

"Now," Powder said, "for reasons best known to myself I get the bright idea to try to apply my program to similar information for some other states. Maybe I'm thinking that the climate is better for guys with no legs elsewhere. I don't know."

Tidmarsh sat.

"Not all other states have the kind of system we've got here, but I manage to get into the records for five other states. Two in the Midwest, two in the Southwest, and one on the West Coast."

"And?"

"And I get life expectancies for all of them that are bigger than the number in Indiana."

"Are the differences statistically significant?"

"That's a little bit gray, because I've had to fudge the comparison in two of the states, but if you take all five of the others together, then the difference between them and Indiana is significant to better than one in a hundred."

"Which is significant," Tidmarsh stated. "How big is the difference in the life expectancies?"

"Eleven months," Powder said.

"Mmmm."

"Now, I am a cranky guy," Powder said. "Did I mention that? Not without considerable charm when I care to trot it out, but I am considered a little nutso by my colleagues."

Tidmarsh's expression indicated a willingness to accept the statement.

"But I am also a pretty fair hand with a microchip, and I spend some time going through what I have already done to try to find some reasonable explanation."

"Is there a difference in the life expectancies between Indiana and these other states for the general population?"

"I take all that into account. In fact, to the best of my knowledge what I have told you has already taken *everything* into account, everything I can think of."

"Well . . ." Tidmarsh said. He leaned back in his chair. "So, why are you likely to die eleven months younger in Indiana than anywhere else?"

Powder's face lit up with his pleasure. "I told you you were good!" he said. "Because I—that's me the computer guy—I've been asking myself the same question. And I couldn't answer it. So what I've done is try to see whether it is just me that's going to die early. I've been working on this one for the last five months."

"When did you do the original work?"

"In the three months before that."

"And what have you got?"

"It's not finished yet. I've only done the three easiest states to compare. Two Midwest and the West Coast."

"But preliminarily?"

"What I am getting is that if I am disabled or a mental patient or in an old people's home I am not going to live as long in Indiana as I will if I live somewhere else."

"By how long?"

"About seven and a half months."

"But significant?"

"Yes. On preliminary findings."

Tidmarsh sat gravely for a moment. "How good a computer man are you, Powder?"

"I'm not capable of judging," Powder said.

"Have you talked to other people about all this?"

"Well, that leads me to my next problem. The information I've been using out of the state data pool is restricted access. And I never had technical clearance for the other Indiana information. And, of course, I haven't been authorized to go hacking into the pools of these other states. But on the other hand, I couldn't just sit on all this, either, not once I really became sure of what I had."

"So?"

"I took a guy at work aside, a guy I could trust, and I talked a bit to him."

"And?"

"Last week I got fired."

"Oh," Tidmarsh said. "Why?"

"Unauthorized everything. Computer time, accessings."

"So you couldn't trust the man you thought you could trust?"

Powder pursed his lips. "So it seems, though it might only be that he alerted someone else accidentally. It's not straightforward because I have this real personality problem that people where I work think I am a joker and a stirrer and a pain in the ass so maybe I wasn't taken seriously."

"So what about your project?"

"Don't ask me how I managed it, but I have all my records and programs and everything I need to continue my work. Except the right mainframe computer."

"What kind of computer would that be?"

"Your kind of computer," Powder said.

"Ah."

The two men sat in silence and stared at each other across the desk that divided them.

"What I am saying," Powder said, "is that I think this guy ought to be seen."

"You've seen him," Tidmarsh said.

"But what do I know? About people, maybe. But not about computers or data pools or tests of statistical significances."

"And suppose his work *is* correct," Tidmarsh said.

"That is something else again," Powder said. "Look. I didn't think I had the right to ignore him."

"I can't conceive how I could get clearance for a civilian to use our mainframe."

"I suppose not. But you'll see him?"

"How did you come across this man, Powder?"

"He reads the papers too."

Tidmarsh frowned.

"He saw Sergeant Fleetwood's picture. Quite apart from having an eye for the ladies, he thought she might have a special interest in a diminished life expectancy for the mobility disabled."

 Howard Haddix, a twenty-five-year-old hypochondriac with red crew-cut hair and a fine moustache, was the only person in the office when Powder returned. He was completing one of the department's "short forms"—for registering someone as missing without initiating a search—and didn't notice Powder's entry at first.

Powder came to Haddix's shoulder and watched his work. He shook his head and made a short sucking sound. "Damn, I wish you were right-handed," he said. "You lefties write so slowly."

"Lieutenant?"

"Yeah?"

"There was a man looking for you five minutes ago. Some kind of lawyer."

"For me? Specifically?"

"He had some kind of envelope and said that it was important that he see you personally. Carollee asked him if it was a subpoena, but he only said it was private business."

"Why didn't he wait?"

"We didn't know how long you'd be gone, so Noble took him to the canteen to get some coffee. The guy said he had some calls to make anyway."

"Where has Fleetwood rolled off to?"

"Detective Day Room. And I think she's going down to the Print Shop after that."

"And Swatts?"

"She wrote whatever it was in the log."

Powder looked in the log and saw that Officer Swatts had gone to County Hospital to look at bodies.

"How's your mother, Haddix?"

"Pretty well, thanks for asking," Haddix said. "But I'm still having these attacks of light-headedness."

"Great," Powder said. He turned to the list of log entries and went through them. "It's been a busy morning."

"Not many we can do much about," Haddix said.

Powder frowned at the concept. "We need more exposure," he said.

"How about a missing persons cable TV station?"

Powder considered the suggestion.

"It was just a thought, Lieutenant."

"Twenty-four hours a day, stories of the people we're looking for. Interviews with the relatives. Celebrations for the ones who come home." Powder rubbed his face with both hands. "You're not as stupid as you look, are you, Howard?"

■ ■ ■

When Noble Perkins, a tall, pale young man of twenty-three with platinum-blond hair, returned to the office, he was alone.

"Thought you were nursemaiding somebody," Powder said.

"I showed him where to get a cup of coffee and left him to drink it," Perkins said.

"It's polite to make conversation with visitors," Powder said.

Perkins wrinkled his nose. "I'm not so hot on conversations."

"You're a stereotype of the computer age, Noble, do you know that?"

"I can't help what I am, Lieutenant, and at least what I am has some things that can do some things."

"True."

"Like, I worked through for that police file you wanted. Sidney Arthur Sweet?"

"What did you get?"

"Nothing. He doesn't have any record of any kind."

"Good," Powder said, feeling predisposed in favor of the kind of man who left notes regularly for his son.

A few minutes later Carollee Fleetwood appeared in the doorway.

"Hey, Powder," she called, "that lawyer with the paternity suit caught up with you yet?"

Back-wheeling quickly, Fleetwood disappeared.

Almost immediately two stout men tried to get through the doorway at the same time. Then they both stepped back and gestured to each other to go first. After a moment, the invitations were accepted and they both stepped forward together again. It looked like a stylish-stout dance routine.

Finally the man in the dark suit persuaded the man in the green flannel shirt to go first.

Powder said in a low voice to Haddix, "Remind me to get the door widened."

The flannel shirt strode up to the counter and said, "Hey, this where I find my uncle?"

"Depends which he is," Powder said affably, looking around the room.

"I got this uncle, see, who quit his house and I want to find him."

"How long ago was this?"

The man squinted in thought. "This was . . . eighteen year and seven month. Yes, seven."

Powder stared at the man. "Was he reported to us as a missing person when he left in the first place?"

"No, no. He just go and leave his wife and his little girl."

"So why are you looking for him now?"

The man drew himself up. "Because his little girl, my cousin, she is getting herself married and we decide in the family that the father ought to know something like that, maybe to give a present to the young couple, help them get started 'cause they're not so well off."

"And what makes you think we can find your uncle after all this time?"

"Hey, I didn't say you can find him. He could be dead or something. But I read in the papers, we got this thing to be proud in Indianapolis, we find more missing people than anywhere else in the Midwest. So we say in the family, hey, we got a missing people. Why not let's try? So that's why I'm here."

"When is the wedding?"

"End of July. We think June first, tradition, but July's more time for arrangements. Now May. No rush, my cousin, you know? A good girl, a real good girl for a father to be proud of and be generous."

Powder turned to Howard Haddix. "Do a long form on it," he said. Then he moved down the counter and looked at the man in the dark suit. The man rose and came to face him.

"Are you Leroy Yount Powder?"

Powder studied the man.

"Are you Leroy Yount Powder?" the man asked again.

"Yes," Powder said.

"Son of Martha Johnson Yount and Brendon Wilson Mallin Powder?"

"Look, what's all this about?"

"Those were your parents' names?"

"Yes."

"I can see that you are a busy man, Mr. Powder. What this is about is that a relative of your late mother's died recently and left you a substantial share of his estate. This letter"—the man produced an envelope from an inside pocket—"explains in full the relationship, details of the bequest, and what happens now. Rather than go into it here, I would ask that you read the contents and then get in touch with me in due course. Let me introduce myself. Jonathan Lindwall."

The man extended his right hand for shaking.

Powder shook it.

The man extended his left hand with the envelope in it.

Powder took it.

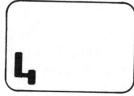

"Give me a break, Lieutenant—it's lunchtime!"

"You're too fat anyway."

The parole officer sighed. "I just cannot give Richard much more latitude. He has become extremely lax regarding the terms of his parole. I have a certain amount of discretion, but I am already past my normal limit. Richard had all the conditions of his parole laid out in plain English and he agreed to meet them. But lately he's missed reporting dates. He's quit his job. I don't even know for certain that he is still living at the address I've got for him. Whenever I call, he's out. There is nothing I *can* do but send him a letter threatening to initiate proceedings to revoke his parole. What the hell do you expect?"

Powder telephoned his ex-wife soon after he left the parole office. He said, "All I could find out is that Ricky has broken several conditions of his parole."

"He hasn't . . . *done* anything, has he?" she asked, her voice bordering on the shrill.

"If he had done anything, I would have said 'Ricky has done something.' The basic problem is that his parole officer—"

"That's that unsympathetic McClarron man?"

"McClarron, yes. McClarron hasn't seen him. Doesn't know where he is."

"He's staying with me!"

"When was the last time you saw him?"

"I see him quite often."

"When was the last time you saw him?"

"Don't you interrogate me, Leroy Powder." After a moment she said, "I talked to him three days ago."

"On the telephone?"

"Well . . ."

"You haven't seen him for, what? A month?"

"Not as long as that."

"Three and a half weeks? It would have helped if you had said so when you told me about the letter. Damn, I should have known. He's been gone so long you're opening his mail now."

"It looked official," she said. "Maybe important."

"You're right," Powder said. "It is important."

"Maybe if you saw McClarron, face to face . . ."

"I did see McClarron face to face and if he doesn't see Ricky face to face the kid's going back to the joint."

"There's no call to use vulgar terms."

"It's a vulgar place."

"Well, what am I supposed to do about it?"

"You can pass the message on. And you can ask our son why the hell he can't do something as simple as show up to see his parole officer once a week."

"He said he thought McClarron would be angry when he found out he had left his job."

"So you knew about that too?"

"They were making life very unpleasant for him there, Leroy."

"More unpleasant than prison?"

"If it wasn't for you, he wouldn't have gone to prison."

"He would have managed to get there all by himself in due time. And a smart kid would have learned enough not to want to go back."

"I would have thought that if anyone should know that all they do in prisons is teach each other different kinds of crimes, it's you."

"That's not all they do in prisons," Powder said quietly. "But I will grant you it doesn't seem to have done him any good."

"If you can admit you made a mistake it will be a pleasant change."

"I didn't say that I made a mistake."

"Typical. You haven't got any heart left at all, have you?"

"Just explain the situation in Dick and Jane words the next time Ricky deigns to telephone you."

"Congratulations, Lieutenant!"

Powder stared at Sue Swatts, a tall, muscular, twenty-two-year-old woman with short brown hair, an engaging smile and an unpolicelike ability to remain cheerful in almost any situation. "What for?"

"I heard at lunch that you just inherited a million dollars or something."

Carollee Fleetwood and Howard Haddix raised their heads. Noble Perkins seemed not to hear.

"Did you now?" Powder asked. "Hey, who told you?"

"It was all over the lunchroom. I heard it from a friend of mine who works in Hit and Run." Swatts narrowed her eyes momentarily. "Is it really true?"

"A rumor in a police department?" Powder asked. "Must be true."

"Gosh," Sue Swatts said. "What you going to do with it? Retire to Florida or something?"

"Gee, Sue," Powder said. "I haven't worked it all out yet, but what I am thinking of doing is going private."

"Private? Private what? I don't understand."

"I mean a special private Missing Persons Department. One not connected with the Police Department, so I can work with people who keep their minds on their business and don't waste all day every day with stupid rumors."

Detective Lieutenant Jerry Miller was filling in an application for promotion when Powder entered his office. Miller glanced up, dropped his eyes back to the form, and then glanced up again. "Powder," he said somberly. He dropped his pen and sighed and leaned back in his chair.

"I filled in one of those once," Powder said. "Take a tip from me. Really sell yourself. Emphasize what you've done. I was too modest—that was my mistake. I ended up in charge of a bunch of kids who are so gullible they'd believe Al Capone if he said he didn't mean to pull the trigger."

"What is it that you want?" Miller asked stonily.

Powder said, "Rumor has it that you have some influence with the CCC cable TV station."

Miller considered before speaking. "I advise them on their

police-related programming. I don't get paid and it's all been cleared by the department."

"Hey, Miller, no need to be defensive with me. I'm not the goddamned promotions board."

Miller waited.

Powder said, "I want you to recommend a new program on missing persons to your people at CCC."

"What, like on how your department works?"

"I mean a regular short program trying to locate missing people."

Miller said nothing.

"Stories and pictures of the people we're trying to find. Interviews with the family left behind. Celebrations when people come home. It's a natural. It'll do even better than pictures of missing kids on milk cartons."

Miller inhaled audibly, then exhaled. "OK," he said. "I'll try it on them. If there's any interest, I'll get back to you."

"Can't ask for more than that," Powder said, rising from the chair he'd dropped into. "So I'll leave and let you get back to *your* daydreams."

When Powder reentered Missing Persons, Fleetwood was interviewing a distraught-looking couple in the booth for private conversations which was separated from the rest of the room by glass partitions.

"What's that?" he asked Haddix.

"Thirteen-year-old girl," Haddix said.

"How long gone?"

"Eight days," Haddix said.

Powder nodded. He went to his desk and sat down. As he did, the telephone rang. The caller was Tidmarsh and when Powder had taken the computer man's short message and hung up, he looked at his watch and made a call of his own.

After five rings the phone was answered and an eager voice said, "Hello? Dad?"

"This is Lieutenant Powder of Missing Persons."

"Oh."

"No practice today?"

"Didn't go," Robert Sweet said.

"Oh," Powder said. Then, "I take it you haven't heard from your father."

"No. Nothing."

"Did you get in touch with your mother's sister?"

"I called her last night after I got back from talking to you. She ain't heard from him for a long time."

"Have you thought of anybody else he might have gone to see? Or any other relatives?"

"Nope."

"Robert, was your father having trouble with anybody?"

"About what?"

"About anything."

"You mean, like, speeding tickets?"

"What kind of trouble was he having about speeding tickets?"

"Just some he didn't pay the fine of once. But he sorted that out."

"I was thinking of other kinds of trouble, with people, or at work or something."

"I can't think of nothing."

"Well, what I want you to do is to make a list of all the people you know of who know your father. Friends first. Then acquaintances. Everybody you know the name of and anything else you know about them."

"This going to find my dad?"

"It might. Will you do that for me?"

"I guess," the boy said.

"All right. Get to work on it, and don't leave anybody out."

"He's dead, isn't he?" the boy said suddenly.

"If you know so much, I'll stop looking for him. Is that what you want?"

"No."

"Did you go to school today?" Powder asked.

"No."

"What are you going to tell them when you go in tomorrow?"

"I can't go in tomorrow."

"Why not?"

"Well I can't get my dad to write me an excuse, can I?"

"Look, kid, you can't let the goddamned world come to an end because your father's gone off somewhere for a few days."

"Easy for you," Sweet snapped. "You didn't just lose your father."

"I've lost a son in my time, kid. So don't go all whiny to me."

At five-thirty Powder and Fleetwood were alone in the office. Powder suddenly leaned back in his chair. The movement attracted her attention and Powder said, "Before I forget, Tidmarsh wants to talk to your chum Mencelli."

"Hey, great," she said. "When?"

"Tomorrow at ten. Think he'll be able to make it?"

"I'll find out."

Powder watched her for several seconds without speaking. Then he said, "You do that."

"Leroy?"

"Yes?"

"What's this stuff about you inheriting money?"

"Come out for a meal. I'll let you count it."

Fleetwood thought for a moment, then said, "Yeah, all right. But I want to get back early."

"What I had in mind was three pizzas in a new place. That OK with you?"

"It wasn't a million dollars then?"

"Wealth brings responsibility. You can't go and spend it. That's not what wealth is for."

■ ■ ■

They used her car. Powder decided on a pizza take-away they had patronized before.

"Don't get out to open the door for me," Powder said as he moved from the passenger seat. "I can manage."

He returned to the car with three pizza boxes and a large bottle of cola.

Fleetwood stared at him as he settled next to her. "What's that stuff for?" she asked, referring to the bottle. "I thought you hated it."

He directed her to an address on Bernard Avenue, a little more than a block from Crown Hill Cemetery.

Fleetwood drove in silence.

"That must be it," Powder said as they cruised slowly, reading the numbers.

She stopped in front of a small house, pebble-dashed with decorative shutters.

"At least there are no stairs."

"Where are we, Powder?"

"I said pizza and I said a new place. Not necessarily connected." He got out of the car, helped her out and they approached the front door with the pizzas.

Robert Sweet answered the doorbell quickly.

"You eaten yet, kid?" Powder asked. But he didn't wait for an answer as he pushed through the doorway. "Take these boxes while I help Carollee in."

Fleetwood dropped Powder back at Police Headquarters at eight-thirty. As he was about to get out of her car, she said, "You didn't tell me about your money."

"Oh, yeah," Powder said. He took the brown envelope he had received from Jonathan Lindwall and passed it to her. "Have a look at that, will you? I haven't had a chance."

Powder did not find the graffiti until after ten when he went to his garage behind the house.

There, on the wall that abutted the path, PIGS EAT SWILL !
was written in phosphorescent-pink spray paint. The light in
the alley behind made the message show up dramatically.

Powder studied the text for a full minute. He rubbed his
face with both hands.

He went into the garage, which had no room for vehicles.
It was adapted for woodwork.

Powder spent an hour on a table designed for a wheelchair
user.

 When Fleetwood arrived in the morn-
ing she asked Powder if he would mind
her spending a little time showing
Jules Mencelli around the Police Department before his ten o'clock appointment with Tidmarsh.

Powder blinked a couple of times and then said, dis-
tractedly, "I don't mind. I'll probably be out by then any-
how."

"Hey, he, we, appreciate you setting this up. And you
know, if there *is* something to it . . ."

"What? Oh, yeah. Keep me in touch."

Fleetwood studied him. "Is something wrong, Powder?"

"No."

Fleetwood made her way to his desk. He watched as she
approached.

She threw the brown envelope he'd given her the night
before toward him. He made no move to catch and it
dropped on the desk surface. "That was still sealed when you
gave it to me."

"I know. I hadn't had time to open it."

"And you don't know what it says?"

"No."

"It says you've inherited a hundred and forty-six thousand dollars. And change."

Powder said nothing for a moment. Then, "How much change?"

"Three hundred and eight dollars and seventy-seven cents. The lawyer can write you a check for it. He's waiting for your instructions."

"Oh."

"Did you know this guy Samuel Yount?"

"Nope."

"Did you know your mother had a half-brother?"

Powder wrinkled his face. "I don't remember things like that anymore."

They looked at each other in silence for a long time.

"Do you know the interest that kind of money could draw?"

"Not offhand."

"With your pension, you could retire in luxury," Fleetwood said.

Powder studied the envelope. He look up at Fleetwood. "I get sunburn," he said.

Powder worked through the details of the day's routine and then decided to talk to Howard Haddix at length. About how to locate the eighteen-years-missing father of the bride-to-be reported the previous day by the man in the green flannel shirt. Anyone who came in and said that Missing Persons was something for Indianapolis to be proud of had to be given a good try.

"A result in this sort of thing is based on drudgery," Powder lectured in summary. "Listing possible sources of information and going through them again and again and again as you broaden your geographical field of search."

Haddix nodded, then felt the back of his neck carefully, as

if making sure nothing had gone wrong there in the course of his indication of agreement.

"But, Howard," Powder said, "you should also follow your impulses. Your feel. Read through the long form on the guy two, three times, every word. Think about what it says about him—like, here, eighteen years ago he was a machinist and he'd been at his job for seven years. Put yourself in his place. Think about what would have taken *you* away abruptly if you'd been him. Call up the people he left behind. Get them to talk to you about him. Get it all together. Then, if you have a feeling about him, a guess what he might have done, don't ignore it. Act on your feeling as well as the drudgery."

"What kind of feeling, Lieutenant?" Haddix asked.

Powder stared at the man.

Then he pushed his swivel chair away from his desk and rose to leave the office.

As Powder got up, Jules Mencelli guided his wheelchair through the department door. "Never fear," he announced. "Your number one man, Ace, is here!"

Fleetwood made her way to the public side of the counter and touched wheels and hands with Mencelli.

"Hey, babe!" he said to her. "How you doing? God, you're beautiful!"

Powder followed through the opened flap in the counter. He said, "I've asked Sergeant Fleetwood to look after you, Mr. Mencelli. Show you around the place a bit until you go up to see Lieutenant Tidmarsh." Powder looked at his watch. "That's a little more than half an hour. You can manage the time, can't you, Sergeant Fleetwood?"

"Sure."

Ace was effusive. "Hey, that's great! Thanks a ton, old fella."

Powder nodded and left the office.

He walked to the stairs and descended to the ground floor, where he proceeded along the corridor to the police garage.

■ ■ ■

At the door of a small, well-maintained ranch-style house on the near-Northeast, Powder showed his police ID to the woman who answered the bell. She glanced at it uninterestedly, as if she'd seen men with such things before. "So what you want?"

"Are you Imelda Nason?"

"Yeah."

"Formerly Imelda Stanton?"

"So?"

"I would like a few words with you and your husband, Mrs. Nason."

The woman, bulky and blond, frowned and hesitated before she said, "You got a warrant?"

"I'm not here to search. I'm not here to arrest anybody. I'm not investigating a crime. I am from the Missing Persons Department and I'm trying to get information about your brother-in-law, Sidney Sweet, who is missing from his home."

"Oh, yeah. The kid, Bobby, he called me. Sorry, I don't know nothing about Sid. I haven't seen him for years."

"That's what Robert told me you'd told him. But you and Mr. Nason are the only family Robert knows the whereabouts of. What I would like is a few minutes talking about what you do know of Sidney Sweet, over the years."

The woman frowned more deeply. "Wait a sec." She closed the door firmly.

Two minutes later the door opened again and Powder faced a short man, thickened by his muscles into the shape of a boulder. He wore a dark-brown suit but no tie. He stepped forward and extended a hand. "Earle Nason," he said.

Powder shook the hand and introduced himself.

"I may have had my troubles with you fellas in the past," Nason said, "ending in me serving seven years of a ten-year sentence for murder two, which ain't no secret. But that was a long time ago and I'm a straight arrow now and I'm always glad to help our friends in blue."

They sat at the kitchen table and Mrs. Nason poured cups of coffee. "Unfortunately," Earle Nason said, "I don't know nothing much about Sid Sweet. I met him a few times when him and Mel's sister Sunny was together, but hardly at all since."

"When did Mrs. Sweet leave?"

"About . . ." Mrs. Nason thought. "It was a December, so that makes it about a year and a half ago."

"Why did she leave?"

The couple looked at each other.

Earle Nason said, "It ain't no secret. She got a smooth Mex boyfriend and they took off, for sunnier parts. Sunnier parts, get it? Sunny?"

"It hadn't been going so good with Sid for a long time before that," Mrs. Nason said. "Sid was real . . ." She squirmed in her chair for the right word, but didn't find it. "Sunny never knew where he was or what he was doing."

"Was he in trouble with the law?" Powder asked.

"No no," Mrs. Nason said. "He was just, well, I don't know. Always edgy, restless, but never doing anything."

"I understand he had a job."

"Oh yeah. But he didn't take his work serious."

"They always seemed to have enough money, though," Earle Nason said.

"True. Not a lot, but plenty, if you know what I mean."

"Do you know where I could get in touch with Mrs. Sweet?"

Both Nasons shook their heads immediately. "We ain't heard from her," Imelda Nason said.

"Before she left were you close to your sister?"

"Not real close. She'd usually call every couple of weeks, but we didn't see ourselves very often."

"She used to come around my place of work sometimes," Earle Nason volunteered.

"What kind of work is that?"

"I am a bodyguard," Nason said with some pride. "And nights I do some bouncing at one of my employer's clubs."

"Who is your employer?"

"Mister Jimmy Husk, what they call Mister Jimmy around town. He's got three clubs and some properties and various other interests and he does everything real gentlemanly, you know? I feel real lucky I've got the good fortune to be working for him, considering my past, because it's steady and it's secure."

"There's not many can say that nowadays," Powder said.

"That's right," Nason said with enthusiasm. "That's what I tell the old lady, don't I, Mel?"

"That's what he tells me," Mrs. Nason said. She did not smile.

"When did you last see Mrs. Sweet?"

"Not since she left," Mrs. Nason said.

"And Mr. Sweet?"

"Must of been more than a year," Earle Nason said. "You remember I ran into him at Leonardo's, Mel. I told you."

Mrs. Nason shrugged.

"Do you have any idea where Mr. Sweet might have gone?"

Nason looked at his wife and back to Powder. He shrugged. "No idea." He turned to his wife.

"I haven't seen the little creep since I can't remember when," Mrs. Nason said.

Sidney Sweet's place of work was a small factory that bottled carbonated drinks. His job involved paper work and some supervision on the line. Although Sweet had worked there for fifteen years, the manager was not particularly interested in the disappearance. Sweet had not reported to work the day he had failed to leave a note for his son, nor had he been seen there since.

Sweet's timekeeping, the manager told Powder, was never good. He was sure Sweet would turn up. The apparent disappearance wasn't important.

Powder found the manager's lack of interest puzzling at best.

 Powder was walking the corridor from the garage to Police Headquarters when a plainclothes detective hailed him and stepped in his way.

"Lieutenant Powder!" the man said. "I planned to come down to see you later today but since fate has crossed our paths, we might just as well take advantage of this little bit of luck. Luck in more ways than one, maybe."

"Do I know you?"

"I don't think so. But let's not wait to be formally introduced. I'm Wayne Killops, detective sergeant. Of course everybody knows you." Killops reached for Powder's right hand, grabbed it, pulled it up from where it dangled by Powder's side, shook it with vigor.

"And," Killops continued, "everybody's heard about your financial good fortune following the unfortunate demise of your relative. Sorry to hear about that, of course, but we're all pleased that a bit of something good has come down to you by way of compensation for your loss."

Powder pulled his hand away.

"What I wanted to talk to you about," Killops continued, "is a vineyard in New Mexico! How about that! You wouldn't expect wine from New Mexico, would you? But it's going to boom like nothing you've ever heard of before, and there are a number of us in the department going together to invest a little money. We stand to make a real killing out of it, a real killing, in the nicest possible sense. So naturally, when the *grape vine* made it clear that you might be in a position to come in, even though almost all the shares are gone, it seemed only right that—"

Sue Swatts was giving her full sympathetic attention to two middle-aged women in flowered dresses when Powder entered the office. Howard Haddix was poised with his left hand over the office log. Fleetwood was on the telephone.

Powder went to Noble Perkins and smacked him on the back.

"Nobe, old buddy, I've been worrying about you."

"Why's that?" Perkins said as he flipped through a fanfold printout.

"Staying in front of that machine all day is going to give you occupational diseases."

The tall young man turned to look up at Powder. "Yeah?"

"Sure as sitting," Powder said. "It's well-documented fact, based on generations of hands-on research with secretaries and typists. It's going to corrupt your hardware and invalidate your software."

"Gosh."

"You've got to make sure to get up and walk around at least ten minutes out of every hour."

Perkins looked a little puzzled. "But where will I go?"

"We'll try to find someplace. How long have you been sitting there this morning?"

Perkins looked sheepish.

"OK," Powder said. "Here, I'll do you a favor. Why don't you go up to auto records and find out what kind of car this man has, and then get a search out for it."

Powder gave Perkins a slip of paper with Sidney Arthur Sweet's name and address on it.

When Fleetwood finally hung up, Powder moved to the edge of her desk. "I am troubled, Sergeant."

"Oh, yeah?" she said, continuing to write on the paper she was working on.

"How much money do bodyguards make?"

"I don't know."

"No? I thought you hired one for a couple of years to fight off all the kinky guys that wanted to touch up your crippled body. Didn't you tell me that once?"

Fleetwood said nothing.

"No, come on. How much bread do bodyguards draw? Enough to buy a house?"

"I guess."

"A nice ranch house with a third of an acre and nice furniture and good clothes?"

Fleetwood shrugged but accepted the doubt that Powder was suggesting.

"And tell me something else. Your average bodyguard, would you expect him to be carrying a gun or not?"

Fleetwood shrugged again.

"Come on! He'd be carrying a gun, wouldn't he, if he were the real thing. So a convicted felon, who wouldn't be licensed to carry, he'd have to be a pretty lucky felon to land himself a secure bodyguarding job, wouldn't he?"

"I don't know any bodyguards, Powder."

"All right. You don't know anything about bodyguards," he said, looking away, affecting patience. "What about that house we had dinner in last night?"

"What are you going to do about that poor kid?"

"Tell me about the house. A nice house?"

"Yeah."

"Worth a bit? More than yours?"

"Yeah."

"Kind of house you could get by working in a bottling plant where they don't rate you and they don't care whether you show up for work or not?"

Powder called a social worker acquaintance for advice about Robert Sweet. Off the record.

"What about the mother?" Adele Buffington asked.

"I don't know where she is," Powder said. "The kid doesn't either. She may be in Mexico somewhere."

"Are there other relatives?"

"All I know of is the mother's sister. None too sympathetic."

"You really ought to report it, Roy."

"The father hasn't even been gone two days yet."

"You sound like you think it's serious though."

"True, it doesn't feel like an ordinary 'Daddy Decamps' to me. But I can't seem to get a handle on it."

"If anything should happen to the boy," Buffington said, "the responsibility would come back to you, in a big way."

"I understand," Powder said.

"What's important is that you try to think of the child."

"When I was over there he hung on to his telephone, like it was a lifeline" Powder said. "If he gets carted out of his own house, what's he going to hang on to?"

Powder went to the canteen and smiled as he saw the angular figure of Lieutenant Tidmarsh drop into a chair at a table next to the windows.

When he'd passed through the line himself, Powder sat down opposite Tidmarsh. "I'd planned to come up to see you later on," he said, "but since fate has crossed our paths I thought I'd take advantage of this bit of luck."

"What a load of bull," Tidmarsh said. "I'm up here this time every day, which you know damn well."

"You computer people," Powder said. "Life by numbers." He took the top off his plain yogurt. "Tell me about Ace Mencelli."

Tidmarsh put down his cup of coffee. He put both arms on the table. He said, "Mencelli knows his business."

"I see," Powder said. "Which means you are going to find some way to let him work?"

"Which means that on the surface of things, by the standards we normally accept here, he has already just about proved his case."

Powder studied his yogurt. "So Indiana is not a healthy place to be disabled?"

"Or mentally ill, or mentally handicapped, or chronically sick."

"Tidmarsh," Powder said, raising his eyes to meet the other man's, "are we talking about what I think we're talking about?"

"Which is?"

"That a substantial number of people in these categories have died younger in Indiana than their counterparts elsewhere for no good reason?"

"That's what we're talking about," Tidmarsh said.

"I see," Powder said.

"What I haven't done is checked the work in detail yet, confirmed the numbers and the formulas. But I've roughed my way through his logic and methodology and if the data he says he's gotten from various places are correct, then it looks pretty strong."

"So it's possible that he's made mistakes?"

"Yes."

"But if he hasn't?"

"Then there is some reason why living in Indiana is unhealthy for certain groups of people."

"What might that be?"

"I can tell you what Mencelli thinks it is."

"Which is?"

"Mencelli thinks there is somebody out there murdering them."

When Powder reentered the office after lunch Sue Swatts asked to consult with him for a moment.

"What can I do for you, Officer Swatts?"

"I was covering the desk for Howard for a while this morning and I had a case I didn't quite know how to handle."

"Was that the floral twins I saw you with?"

"Floral . . . ?" A questioning smile.

"Two women wearing dresses made out of the same material with flowers on it."

"Oh!" with recognition. "No, no. They were just asking directions to Municipal Courtroom Five. They were witnesses."

"Pity. I thought they'd come in to report the third triplet had run away and was suspected of wearing plaids."

Swatts nodded gently as she tried to make sense of his comment.

"Do you *always* smile?" Powder asked.

"Gee, I guess my face just kind of rests in that shape, Lieutenant." She giggled momentarily. "It's always been like that."

"It's not natural."

"It's not?" Still smiling.

"You wanted to ask me something," Powder said tiredly.

"Oh. Yeah, what I wanted to know is what we do about parents who report a daughter missing and they know where she is."

"Some details, please."

"I had this couple come in wanting us to get their daughter out of some group called The Promised Land."

"Not one of those boring cult things . . . ?"

"Afraid so."

"How old is the girl?"

"Nineteen."

"And where is The Promised Land?"

"There's a farm off Moore Road."

"Where's that?"

"Near the Boone County border. On Big Eagle Creek."

Powder rubbed his face with both hands. He said, "If the parents know where the daughter is, she's not a Missing Persons case."

"They didn't get any help when they went upstairs," Swatts said. "They were sent to us because the girl is so old."

"Send us your weak, your lame, your halt and your over-sixteens."

"Excuse me?"

"Not many people would confuse Indianapolis with the promised land," Powder said. "Still, I suppose it's getting pretty crowded in the cult business these days."

Swatts stood looking at Powder for a moment.

"Do you *want* something, Officer?"

"The parents seemed so sad."

"Parenthood is intrinsically sad," Powder said.

Swatts shrugged. "Is it?"

"What else of interest happened this morning?" Powder asked.

"I managed to match a body. A hit and run with a man on 'Have You Seen Them?' who went out for a video movie and didn't come back."

"Good. How about letting the press know?"

Fleetwood was the last back after the lunch break.

She came to Powder's desk and said, "Jules thinks he is going to get some computer time here."

"He's still around?"

"I just saw him off. I took him to lunch."

"Lucky Jules."

"Jules thinks Tidmarsh was impressed."

"Jules has a pretty good opinion of himself," Powder said.

"Tidmarsh wanted to go through some of the work in more detail. Jules will probably be asked back in tomorrow."

"I'll try to make sure you're free," Powder said. He turned away, rose and walked to Noble Perkins's computer corner.

"How are you feeling, Noble?"

"OK, I guess, sir. You got my message?"

"Which message was that?"

"That the car you wanted hasn't been found?"

"Yes, I got that all right."

"OK. Good," Perkins said.

"Did you have some lunch?"

"Yes, sir."

"Did you get out of your chair and walk someplace for it?"

"I went to the canteen."

"Good work, Noble. You'll feel the benefit."

"I feel OK now, sir."

Powder sat at his own telephone and called the Sweets' home number.

After two rings Robert Sweet answered. "Hello. Dad?"

"I wrote you a note last night so that you could go back to school today."

"Oh, it's you."

"Do you understand, son, that if you play truant it will be taken as evidence that you can't cope alone while your father is away and the city will move you out of your house?"

"They can't do that!"

"They can do that," Powder said.

"Who would answer the phone?"

"Your father wouldn't call at this time of day anyway," Powder said. "He didn't bring you up to skip off school."

"He didn't mind sometimes," the boy said. "He's all right that way, my dad."

Powder sat in thought at his desk. After a time he wrote out the name and address of the bottling plant Sweet had worked at on a piece of paper. Then he added the names Earle Nason, Imelda Nason née Stanton, "Sunny" Sweet née Stanton.

He took his list to Noble Perkins.

"I want whatever is in the data bank on these names, as a priority," Powder said.

"I'm going out," Fleetwood said.

The voice broke Powder's concentration.

Fleetwood watched as he raised his eyes and took her in.

"I just don't get it," Powder said. "A guy who really works at being a father just disappears one day. No contact with the kid. Why?"

"I take it you didn't get anything useful from the sister-in-law."

Powder shook his head.

"On the list the son made for you there weren't any friends, were there?"

"No."

"Isn't that a little odd?"

"Yes."

"What did this man do for adult company?" Fleetwood asked.

"Mmmm," Powder said uneasily. "I don't know."

"Which means either he had no 'own' life or he kept it secret."

"Yes," Powder said. "What are you doing tonight?"

"I'm going over to see Jules. Sorry."

"When there's work to be done?" Powder asked in an offended tone.

■ ■ ■

When Noble Perkins gave Powder printouts of the information he had obtained on the East Haven Bottling Company, the Nasons and "Sunny" Stanton Sweet, Powder folded them and put them in a pocket. He rose to leave for the day.

But as he did, a large man in dungarees entered the office and approached the counter where Sue Swatts and Howard Haddix sat working. He chose to address Swatts and fixed her with a gaze of unwavering intensity. "My name is Gale Heyhurst. I am from The Promised Land."

"Oh," Officer Swatts said.

Powder stepped to the counter. "We have a complaint this morning from the parents of one of your recruits."

Heyhurst took a moment to detach his attention from Sue Swatts. Then, speaking in a low, soft voice, he said to Powder, "So I understand. I have come in to make clear that they are free to visit their daughter at any time. It would be helpful if they were to give a little notice, but it is not necessary. Here is a map of how to get to us. If one hasn't been to us before, it can be a little difficult to find."

Powder took the folded paper that the man offered. "A map to The Promised Land," Powder said.

"Just so," Heyhurst said.

"Tell me," Powder said, "when I inform Mr. and Mrs. ..." He looked in the log for the names. "Mr. and Mrs. Beehler and pass this on to them, can I assure them that they'll be able to see their daughter alone?"

"In private," Heyhurst said. "Certainly." His concentration on Powder increased and he said, "In The Promised Land we have no need for the techniques of group influence."

"Usually called brainwashing."

"We depend on the cogency of our reasoning."

"Got a lot of sheep in your flock, Mr. Heyhurst?"

"We are a thriving, growing community. We enjoy life and we look foward to the future."

"Would you object to my asking for a concise statement of what principles are at the core of your beliefs?"

"We believe," Heyhurst said, "in the restructuring of American society, by means of the electoral process. Our motivating force is enlightened self-interest."

Powder scratched his head. "Enlightened self-interest?"

"We call it ESI."

"Does that mean you're in it for the profit?"

"Yes," Gale Heyhurst said, staring hard at Powder, but not without a suggestion of humor in his expression.

"Oh," Powder said. "Good stuff. I'll pass the message on."

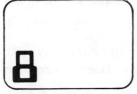

Powder went from work to his neighborhood grocery, Johnson's. A focus of civic activities, centered on the Johnson family's paterfamilias, the store was far more than a source of food. But this time Powder simply assembled a collection of frozen meals. Then he went to Robert Sweet's house.

When the boy answered the door he said, "Oh, I thought it was Dad."

Powder scowled. "Would your father ring the bell?"

"Might have lost his key."

"Look, kid, chances are your father *isn't* coming back. The sooner you stop mooning around and drooling at every creak of a floorboard, the better. Now, how are you off for money?"

The boy was silent.

"Do you have any money?" Powder insisted.

"Not really."

"What the hell does that mean?"

"I've got about a buck and a half."

"OK." Powder gave the boy twenty dollars. "Tomorrow, after *school*, you get yourself something. Anything. A magazine, a comic, some baseball chewing gum. Now, there's some frozen food in this bag. Shall we get it unpacked before I have to be treated for frostbite?"

They went to Sweet's kitchen, and Powder watched as the boy loaded the freezer section of his refrigerator. Then the two of them sat down at the kitchen table.

"Your father has been gone for at least fifty hours and we don't know where or why. His car is gone but hasn't been recovered in this state as abandoned. He gave neither you nor his employer warning that he was going or information where he would be. That much we know, right?"

"Right."

"Did he give you any idea, either in what he said or the way he acted, that anything was different the few days before he left?"

The boy shook his head.

"Nothing at all? He wasn't extra nice to you, or nervous, or out of the house more than usual or at home more than usual?"

"No."

"You're sure?"

"I've been thinking about it a lot."

Powder nodded. "Then the most probable explanation is that something happened that surprised him. Chances are it wasn't an accident in Indianapolis, because of the car and because I have checked the hospitals and he isn't in any of them. But something might have happened out of town. Do you know of any place outside the city where he ever went?"

The boy shook his head.

"Or where he had any relatives, or friends, even ones he never visited?"

"No."

"All right," Powder said, and he took out his notebook. "We will do a check on all the hospitals in the state." He made a note. "Now," he said, "it's possible that he got into some other kind of trouble."

"You mean like somebody kidnapped him?"

"Do you have any reason to believe that somebody might have kidnapped your father?"

"No," the boy said.

"No call from anybody about him?"

"No, no," Robert Sweet said. "I was just thinking. It was a stupid idea."

"All right," Powder said. "When you made me a list of people your father knew . . ."

"Yeah?"

"There weren't any women on it. Is he gay or do you just not know about his social life?"

"I . . . I don't know."

"He didn't talk about socializing?"

"No."

"But he was out in the evening sometimes?"

"Yeah. He leaves me notes."

"How often in a week was he out evenings?"

"Maybe twice, three times."

"Out of seven days?"

"Yeah."

"Any regular days each week?"

The boy considered. He shook his head.

"Where did he say he was going?"

"Just out. I always thought it was, like, work."

"His employer says that he worked a five-day week, eight to five."

"But he was home sometimes."

"When?"

"In the mornings or sometimes when I got back from school."

"How often?"

"Pretty often."

"How often?"

"Oh, once or twice every week."

"Or three times?"

The boy nodded.

"And he was out weekend days sometimes?"

"Yeah."

"But you don't know what he did then?"

"No."

"What do *you* do when he's out?"

"Oh, I'm OK. I'm used to looking after myself."

"Did he leave you money when he went out?"

"Usually."

Powder felt tired. But continuing, he said, "Social life. Did your father *ever* talk about women?"

"Like, specific women?"

"OK."

"No."

"Did he like women? Did he comment on them on TV or in the movies or pictures in the papers? Did he talk about them in general?"

"Well, some I guess."

"Did he ask you about your social life? Tease you about girl friends?"

"A little."

"Did the two of you talk much?"

"What about?"

"Anything."

"Oh, yeah. Quite a bit."

"What about?"

"Well, we talk about baseball a lot. My dad knows a hell of a lot about baseball. Who did what and when. He knows all about the Indians."

"You went to games together?"

"Sometimes, but we watched them on TV more."

"Did he come to see you play? In Little League?"

"Yeah. He watches, when he can."

"What position do you play?"

"I'm a second baseman."

"Are you good?"

The boy shrugged. "Good glove, no hit."

"There's always a place for a good glove at second base," Powder said.

The boy stared at the table.

"You've missed two practices?"

"Yeah."

"I'll write you another note, to get you back into school without fuss."

"OK." Then, eventually, "Thanks."

"Robert," Powder said, "this is a nice house."

The boy nodded, watching him.

"But your dad didn't earn enough at his job to pay for it."

"He doesn't have to pay for it," Sweet said.

"Why not?"

"He owns it."

"Outright? No mortgage?"

"Yeah."

"How do you know?"

"He says so. Sometimes he says, 'At least I own my own house.' "

"Where'd he get the money?"

"I don't know."

"You've always lived here?"

"Uh huh."

"How old are you?"

"Twelve."

"And your mother left about a year and a half ago?"

Eyes down. "That's right."

"Have you seen her since?"

"No."

"But you hear from her sometimes."

"I used to get presents."

"When was the last one?"

"Christmas. She was in Mexico then. She sent me a sombrero and a big silver belt buckle."

"What did your father think about that?"

"It made him sad."

"OK, kid," Powder said. "Now what I need is a picture of your father."

"I don't have one. He doesn't like them."

"No picture of any kind?"

"I don't know of any."

Powder frowned. But took a breath and said, "The other thing I need is to go through his papers. Financial records, letters, all that kind of thing. If you let me I'll take them home, but if you don't want me to do that, I'll go through them here."

The boy thought for a long time.

"I know," Powder said, "that he wouldn't like anybody going through them. But if I'm going to try hard to find him, then I think I really have to."

"Take them," Sweet said, "I don't care."

"You show me where they are. And if you don't mind, I'll have a look around the house at the same time."

"All right." The boy paused. Then he said, "You don't think he could have amnesia or something like that?"

"It's possible, Robert," Powder said. "But in all the years I've been a policeman the only real amnesia cases I've seen have been the ones on television."

Powder spent more than an hour looking around the house and gathering Sidney Sweet's papers in a cardboard box. While he did so, Robert put two TV dinners in the oven to heat.

After they had eaten, Powder sat with Robert Sweet and played Old Maid for three quarters of an hour. He left the boy at about nine-thirty to go home.

■   ■   ■

As he carried the box of papers from his car to his own front door Powder saw that his front window was broken.

He stood and looked at it.

Then he continued up the path.

Inside, among the scattered fragments of glass, he found a stone. First he checked through his rooms to make sure nothing had been stolen. Then he brushed and vacuumed until he was satisfied the glass was gathered. In his workshop he found a piece of plywood to fit the pane and cut it to size. He took it back to the house and fixed it in place.

He threw the stone away.

When Powder arrived at the office in the morning, Fleetwood was already there.

So was Jules Mencelli.

To Fleetwood, Powder said, "What's *he* doing here at this time of day?" But before she could reply, Powder turned to Mencelli, saying, "This office is not yet open."

"Look, Powder—" Fleetwood began.

"Why the hell don't you become a *missing* person, Mencelli?"

"What did I say? What did I say?"

"Don't pay any attention, Jules."

"Pay attention," Powder said sharply. "What do you think? I make noises just to feel the rush of air between the gaps in my teeth?"

"Powder, we want to talk."

"Just keep your voices down so you don't bother the working people around here."

"About business."

"Whose?"

"Yours. Ours. Police business."

Fleetwood raised the flap for him. Sourly Powder passed to his desk.

"Jules and I went through it all again last night," Fleetwood said.

Powder said nothing.

"About his work. About what is happening."

"Have we decided to accept that something is happening?"

"Tidmarsh accepts it."

"Tidmarsh is checking your friend's work for mistakes."

"There aren't any mistakes," Mencelli said. "I'd bet my life on it."

"So, in life terms," Powder said, "you lose either way."

"Having talked about it—" Fleetwood said.

"I understand that you've talked about it," Powder snapped. "Are you going to tell me a third time? What the hell is the bottom line around here? Is anybody going to get to it? If not, I have work to do."

Fleetwood tilted forward in her wheel chair, balancing on her hands and looking furious. "Put a zipper on it, Leroy," she said. "I don't have spare time either, especially not for one of your tantrums."

Jules Mencelli smirked. Ostentatiously he put a hand over his mouth to cover his smile.

Powder rubbed his face.

"Bottom line," Fleetwood said. "We shouldn't sit around on Jules' conclusion."

"Which is?"

"That somebody is killing people."

"OK. You think the case is ready? Go to Captain Gartland with it. He's your man, I think."

"What I wanted to do was talk to you about it."

"Gartland will talk to you. He likes talking to policewomen, especially ones with big chests. Good thing he's not a leg man."

"Are you incapable of being constructive this morning?"

"You want permission to work on the case? I give you permission. How much more constructive can I be?"

"You can tell us what *you* think might actually be happening."

"What *I* think is happening?" Powder pursed his lips and leaned back in his chair. "I think that you and Ace here have got yourself swept up in the excitement of a mutual admiration and that you are trying to run before you can jointly walk. That's what I think. I also think that when Tidmarsh says the work is sound and asks what I think about it, then maybe I'll jog my brain cells. But I won't even put a sweat suit on them for Jules." He leaned forward. "Anything else I can do for you this morning, Sergeant?"

Powder sat brooding at his desk after Fleetwood and Mencelli left the office. He pushed pieces of paper from one location to another. He considered momentarily whether immediate action on Mencelli's hypothesis *was* appropriate. But he concluded quickly that it wasn't. He was satisfied with his decision. And then he was simultaneously dissatisfied with it.

There was a lot of early activity in the office. Powder managed to dredge up enough civility to deal with a few of the people who came in. But he was nearer the edge on the routine phone calls which, to help Haddix, he made between conversations with visitors to the counter. These were the contacts with relatives at defined intervals after the initial filing of a missing person report, on cases the department itself was not making headway with. Sometimes the relatives had remembered or received additional useful information. Sometimes the missing person had come home. The relatives by no means always informed the department.

Powder made a dozen calls before he realized that he was coming across as tired and irritated. That was because he was irritated, and, probably, tired. He didn't know what to do about it.

During the morning Noble Perkins checked hospitals throughout Indiana and in the big cities near Indiana— Chicago, Detroit, Columbus, Cincinnati, Louisville—for bodies or unidentified patients who might be Sidney Arthur Sweet. Perkins's initial contacts turned up three possible corpses, and photographs were requested via a telephone printer.

By way of Noble Perkins, Powder also sent a glass, a library book, and an electric razor to Forensic—articles likely to bear Sweet's fingerprints—which he'd removed from the house along with the personal papers. He told Noble Perkins to tell Forensic it was urgent.

When Perkins came back he said that the Forensic people had said all their work was urgent. Powder called the department and told them that the future of a twelve-year-old child depended on their doing quickly what he had asked them to do.

"Sure, sure," the officer in Forensic had said, unimpressed. Powder hung up on him.

When he gave up on telephone calls, Powder spent a little time going through Sweet's papers. In this first look he found only confirmations of what the son had told him. No mortgage or rent records. The house appeared to be his own.

Before lunch Powder put Perkins on finding out who Sweet had bought the house from and when.

Tidmarsh was not in the cafeteria when Powder arrived. That fact increased Powder's already substantial annoyance with life. Too many things to do; all of them complicated, complicated, complicated.

He collected a pastry, a doughnut, and a piece of apple pie

with ice cream, picked up two cups of coffee. He paid and
went to a window table in a corner where he could see everyone in the room. But instead of watching the people in the
room he looked out the window, at the Market Square
Arena parking lot, the sidewalks on Alabama. Buses. An
electric company repair project blocking traffic in the far
side's curb lane. The vehicles clogged the flow of traffic at
the repair site. Powder looked down and thought in terms of
washing machine waste-water pipes and blockages and
plumbers with flexible rods.

He sighed. He rubbed his face.

"Your ice cream's melting, Powder."

"What?"

Tidmarsh stood across the table smirking down at him, a
bean pole of a man with a relief-map face.

"It's making a puddle on your tray."

Powder looked at the ice cream. He pushed the tray, the
food, away. "I'm on a diet," he said. Then, "Tidmarsh, you
used to be in traffic, right?"

"Yes."

"Look down there."

Tidmarsh looked.

"The way traffic flow is blocked."

"I see it."

"Why the *hell* do they put the manhole covers in the
streets, tell me that. If they put them in the sidewalks, then
you could do your work without making the vehicle flow a
mess."

Tidmarsh sat down. "You kill me, Powder, you really do.
How does somebody as temperamental as you stick it as a
cop all the years you have?"

"Temperamental? ¿*Yo*?"

Tidmarsh unloaded his lunch, spread a napkin on his lap
and applied condiments to several of his purchases.

"Do you think you can deny yourself tomato syrup long
enough to tell me whether this guy Mencelli is any good?"

Tidmarsh gently tapped the bottom of the ketchup bottle over his French fries and then over a helping of creamed corn. "It needs more confirming."

"I thought you were doing that."

"I picked out a section and obtained some of his data myself. They all checked exactly. But it was a fraction of the work as a whole."

"What's the bottom line, Tidmarsh?"

"There is no bottom line, yet."

"But suppose you had to put your money on whether it will hold up."

"I'm not really a gambling man, Powder."

Powder glared.

Somberly Tidmarsh ate three French fries. "My gut feeling is that Indiana has a problem to solve."

"Indiana? Who's that?"

Tidmarsh shrugged. "I don't know, my friend. Depends just what kind of problem it is." He shook his head while keeping his fork hand steady. "It's hard to believe. It really is."

"Would you be able to sell it as a case to open to, say, Gartland?"

Tidmarsh did not respond immediately.

"Or to the state cops? Do you know anybody over there?"

"Nobody with clout." Tidmarsh paused, then said, "The trouble with someone like Gartland is he's going to want to know what exactly we're trying to solve, what our jurisdiction is, how much it's going to cost, how many people it will take and for how long."

"To which you say?"

"I can't tell him any of those things yet."

"And presumably," Powder said, "there is also a political aspect. Not good advertising for the state if, when, it hits the press."

"Or for the State Health Department officials."

"So, suppose we decide somebody *is* bumping people off," Powder said. "To get the statistical effect Mencelli's turned up, how many people has he had to kill?'"

Tidmarsh pondered. He made gestures.

Impatiently Powder said, "I *know* it depends on how long he's been at it and fifteen point eight other things but give me a number to think about."

"Several hundreds, maybe a thousand odd. That's a minimum kind of guess. I'll work out a real estimate once I've confirmed Mencelli's work." He thought. "Maybe I'll do it first."

"You're going to go through more of it?"

"It must all be checked," Tidmarsh said forcefully. "Something like this? You can't possibly do anything with it until it's all been confirmed, independently."

"Meanwhile . . ."

"Meanwhile more people are being killed, *if* it's correct. *If.* Jesus, Powder, it *can't* be true!"

"So you will do the checking yourself?"

Tidmarsh ate again. "Who else? I'm the best we've got."

"Ah, Carollee, my dear," Powder said when he returned to the office from the canteen. "How nice to see you."

Fleetwood looked up.

"I wanted to talk something over with you, if you have a minute." Powder sat on the edge of her desk.

Fleetwood said nothing.

"Suppose there is this man who kills aged and infirm people over a period of years. A lot of people, at least a thousand. Maybe several thousand. I know such a thing is absurd, and hardly the sort of activity a beautiful and charming young woman would normally speculate about. But consider it with me for a moment, all right?"

Fleetwood remained silent but looked stern.

"I'll tell you the thing that puzzles me, once we've agreed

to think about such a man. How the hell does he go about it? How does he find appropriate targets? How does he decide when?"

"Powder, you are the most irritating human being I have ever known."

"Flattery aside, how does he do it? I mean, if he runs out and lines the residents in a nursing home up against the wall and uses a machine gun, someone might notice. So what is the rationale, the method? *I* think it's got to be things like fires and explosions because to get through that number you can hardly take them on one at a time." Powder paused, tilting his head to consider. "Unless that's part of the kick involved."

"Excuse me. Lieutenant Powder?" A woman's voice came from behind them.

"Your public calls," Fleetwood said.

"Well, Carollee, you do your best with the little problem I've set you," Powder said. "I'm sure if you think it through carefully, you'll end up a better cop for the effort."

He turned to the counter. "Miss, what can I do for you?"

"It's 'Mrs.' " The woman was short, well dressed, in her early fifties and had a pleasant face.

"Mrs. Forgive me."

The woman pushed her face forward, with something of an ironic smile in her expression. "Don't you recognize me, Roy Powder?"

Powder blinked.

The woman looked past him to Fleetwood and shook her head gently. "How do you like that?" she said. "Here I am, the first woman he ever took to bed, and he doesn't even remember!"

"I'd never have believed he could blush," Fleetwood said to Sue Swatts. "But I am an eyewitness." Fleetwood raised her voice. "Got that, Powder? I'll testify you blushed deep-purple, all the way to the Supreme Court."

Swatts looked over to the desk where Powder was leaning back in his chair, apparently in thought. "Oh, poor man," Swatts said sympathetically. Suddenly her shoulders rose and her face became an agony of pleasure. She was stifling laughter.

Fleetwood snorted. "Yeah, I suppose he is."

"But what did she want, this woman?"

"She said she had seen something strange—"

"But not recently!" Swatts interrupted, giggling.

Fleetwood giggled too.

"Oh dear," Swatts said. "I'm sorry. I shouldn't." She glanced again at the seemingly imperturbable Powder. He had not moved from his contemplative position. "Go on."

Fleetwood and Swatts looked at each other and after a moment broke into laughter again.

"I think we better get some coffee," Fleetwood said.

The two women made their way to the office door. As they did, Howard Haddix arrived and stood aside for them. Looking at Haddix, they burst into laughter once again.

"What's the matter with them?" Haddix asked Powder as he came in.

From his computer corner, Noble Perkins turned and said sharply, "They're being damned silly!"

Perkins's highly uncharacteristic interjection drew even Powder's attention. He and Haddix exchanged raised eyebrows.

Perkins saw the two men look at him. "Women!" he said, by way of explaining his previous comment. He began to turn red. He returned to his VDT.

Powder said, "Howard, you're an intelligent man."

"I am?"

"I've begun to appreciate your perceptiveness lately. I'd like your opinion on something. Come here; sit down."

Haddix sat down.

"A woman comes into some cash when her only brother dies and decides to buy a house with it. One she can rent part of out."

"Yes . . . ?"

"So she gets it all set up and sorted out and furnished and she finds a tenant. Are you with me so far?"

"Yes," Haddix said, and then felt stupid for answering a stupid question.

"The guy that rents it seems all right. Pays in advance. Doesn't cause any trouble, but after a while the woman notices that he keeps odd hours and spends most days in his room."

After a pause, Haddix saw that Powder wasn't going to continue without a prompt. "Yes," he said.

"So the woman doesn't know what to think and it worries her. *Then* the woman remembers that she knows a cop. She hasn't been in touch with him for a long time but she's seen references to him in the papers."

"So she asks the cop about the man?" Haddix asked.

"Exactly!" Powder said. "And invites him to come over for a look, maybe a bite to eat. Nothing so strange or suspicious about that, is there?"

Haddix shrugged. "Nope. Sounds quite reasonable to me."

"My feelings exactly," Powder said. His face, however, remained wrinkled in a frown of dissatisfaction.

"Is this what just happened, Lieutenant? Are you the cop?"

"I said you were intelligent, Howard. You haven't let me down."

But," Haddix said, looking around for Swatts and Fleetwood, "I still don't see what's so funny."

In the early afternoon Noble Perkins gave Powder a printout on the ownership history of Sidney Sweet's Bernard Avenue house. It showed Sweet as having owned the house for fourteen years. There was nothing in the record that suggested any family relationship between the previous owner and Sweet, nothing to explain a mortgageless purchase.

Powder asked Perkins to try to locate the previous owner of the house, one Morris Kijovsky.

Then Powder remembered the other sheets of paper he had been given nearly twenty-four hours before. They were where he had put them, in his jacket pocket.

He considered why he had neglected them, then remembered he had planned to study them at home the previous night. But he had spent the allotted time sweeping up glass and boarding his window instead. Then this morning he'd forgotten them because of his mood.

Powder took the papers out and studied them.

The first was a short résumé on the East Haven Bottling Company, Sweet's employers. The summary showed that while the business held a number of small bottling contracts, their mainstay was a long-standing agreement to supply own-brand carbonated drinks to state and federal institutions of a wide variety of kinds. East Haven's listed owner was another company called Leisure Services. There were no profit-and-loss figures.

Powder took the sheet to Noble Perkins.

"Yes, Lieutenant?"

"Where'd you get this stuff?"

Perkins smiled faintly. "Well, you know the brokers O'Nions and James?"

Powder held up a hand to forestall further explanation. "And the reason you don't know if East Haven is making money is . . . ?"

"It's not incorporated."

"So how about something on Leisure Services?"

"I already tried. O'Nions and James don't have anything on them."

Powder frowned. "Is that unusual?"

"I reckon it is, though I don't know all that much about routines in accountancy."

Powder looked then at the short files on the Stanton sisters. Sunny, whose birth certificate name was Bettina, had been questioned twice—at seventeen and eighteen years of age—because she had been in the company of men arrested for felonies, but she had no criminal record of her own.

From her birth date, Powder worked out that she had married Sidney Sweet when she was nineteen.

Imelda Stanton was the elder sister and the better known to the police. She had only one conviction, for solicitation—a charge she had pleaded not guilty to—but she had been considered a regular associate of criminals until her marriage to Earle Nason at the age of twenty-four, sixteen years before.

Nason, in turn, had a substantial criminal record. Several juvenile and minor adult theft offenses had preceded three assault convictions and two short stays in jail. Then Nason had been convicted of second-degree murder, two years after his marriage. Since his release there had been no further arrests.

The murder conviction had come from a killing committed in the course of a bank robbery. Nason had become agitated and pulled the trigger of the shotgun he was carrying. Although he had not, apparently, intended to shoot, a man had died.

The victim's name was Arnold Husk. He was listed as the proprietor of a club called Leonardo's and two other businesses.

Powder read through the details of Nason's record twice. Then he went again to Noble Perkins, asking this time for further information on Arnold Husk, and on "Mister Jimmy" Husk, Earle Nason's current employer.

Powder's attention turned to Sidney Sweet's personal papers. These he went through sheet by sheet, finding them to be primarily skimpy tax-related records which told him only that Sweet had been earning a comfortable living from his efforts at the East Haven Bottling Company, considering he did not have to pay for accommodation.

There was nothing personal. Powder had hoped for letters or a book of telephone numbers. But he didn't get anything like that, not an old shopping list or check stubs or even the names of Sweet's doctor or dentist.

The longer he looked at the papers the more uncomfortable Powder became. It was possible, he supposed, that Sweet had removed all personal records before he left, but that was not the impression Powder had received when he'd collected the papers into the box.

Powder's problem was that the close and personal relationship that the boy described having with his father was at odds with the impersonal leavings of the father, just as the assiduous note-writing was at odds with the disappearance.

Powder didn't know what he was looking for, only that he wasn't finding it.

When he finished, he repacked the papers.

At four o'clock Noble Perkins presented Powder with pictures of three corpses and a telephone number for a Morris

Kijovsky. Powder put the pictures on top of the box of Sweet's documents and dialed the number.

Kijovsky was in. "You're lucky to catch me," he said. "Was it about some insurance?"

Powder explained who he was. Kijovsky explained that he was an insurance salesman.

"What I wanted to know is whether you remember selling your house on Bernard Avenue."

"Sure I do," Kijovsky said without hesitation. "It was the first house I ever bought, and the first one I ever sold. What about it?"

"Do you remember the man you sold it to?"

"A guy named Sweet. Big guy, built lke a basketball player gone to seed, you know what I mean?"

"Sidney Sweet?"

"I think Sidney. Don't recall his first name so sharp."

"But he was definitely a large man? Not small and nervous?"

"I don't think anybody could call the man who bought my house small," Kijovsky said. "And he wasn't nervous. I was the one that was nervous, that he would change his mind as sudden as he made it up. What's this all about? Or is that something you can't tell me?"

"I am trying to get some background information on a Missing Persons case, Mr. Kijovsky," Powder said. "Can you tell me how long it was between Mr. Sweet showing an interest and his buying?"

"No time at all. A week. He came out and we talked about how fast I could move, which was very fast. He sent a surveyor around the next day and I was gone seven days later. He even paid my price, no haggling. I'm not going to forget that, now am I?"

"No," Powder agreed.

"Who is it that's missing? I know it's none of my business, but—"

"Mr. Sweet is missing," Powder said.

"Gee," Kijovsky said. "You guys are quick off the mark, aren't you?"

"What do you mean, Mr. Kijovsky?"

"Well, I only saw him on the street yesterday."

"Where was that?" Powder asked sharply.

"It was just on the street. On The Circle. I passed him. I've seen him eight or ten times over the years. He never recalled me, but I recall him. I'm pretty good on faces and names, which is an asset in my line of work. It's recalling telephone numbers I have trouble with."

"The times you've seen him, Mr. Kijovsky, where have they been?"

"Oh, just around town."

"It could be very important. Can you remember seeing him coming in or out of any particular buildings? Or any other details at all?"

"That's a pretty tall order," Kijovsky said. "I'd have to think about that one."

"I would be very grateful if you would do that," Powder said. "And I would also appreciate it if you would help a police artist make a sketch of the man you saw yesterday."

Kijovsky recognized the sense of urgency in Powder's voice. "Yeah," he said, "well, OK."

"I'll try to arrange for someone to come out to where you are. Could you wait there now?"

Powder tried to book an artist to go out immediately.

"Sorry, no can do."

"Oh yes you damn well can," Powder said.

The artist agreed to appear at the Missing Persons office at five. Powder called Kijovsky back to fix a meeting for five-thirty.

"This artist couldn't do with some insurance, could he?" Kijovsky asked.

■ ■ ■

A few minutes before five a man and a woman rushed through the door and up to the desk.

The woman dropped her purse on the counter heavily and said, "We went exactly where the map we got from your Miss Swatts said, but she still wasn't there!"

"Something's got to be done about these people," the man said. He pounded on the counter with his fist. "I don't mean just because of Jacqueline either. They are a blot on the landscape, and you people shouldn't just let them spirit hardworking families' daughters away without so much as a by-your-leave."

"Don't bang on my counter top," Powder said.

"What?" the man said.

"I said I will not have you banging on my counter top. Now, do you want to tell me what your problem is, quietly, or would you rather leave?"

The man and woman looked at each other.

"I want to see whoever is in charge here," the man said.

"I am in charge here," Powder said.

"I object to your attitude," the man said.

Powder turned to the office log and wrote a few words.

"What are you doing?" the man asked.

"Noting your objection to my attitude," Powder said. He turned back to the couple. "Now, am I to take it that you paid a visit to The Promised Land?"

The woman burst into tears.

Powder listened to the Beehlers' story, which included the possible ruin of two shock absorbers on the rocky track from Moore Road to the "X" on the map. From what Powder could make out, Gale Heyhurst had been apologetic when he told them their daughter was not at the farm. When they had asked him where she was, Heyhurst had told them she was going door to door spreading the message of the movement. If they cared to fix a time and a day, he could see that Jacqueline was available to them.

"Imagine how we felt," Beehler said stormily. "Making an appointment with this, this . . ."

"A guru type," Mrs. Beehler said.

"Yes, a goddamn guru-hippy-freak, he's standing there with a Snoopy diary in his hand and he's leafing through the pages and he's telling us to make an appointment to see our own daughter."

On the word *daughter*, Mrs. Beehler burst into tears again.

Noting that Officer Swatts was not in the office at the moment, Powder was unable to promise immediate action on the case, but Mr. Beehler produced the map to The Promised Land when Powder asked for it and Powder made a photocopy. The act seemed to calm the couple a little and they left.

Morris Kijovsky was regretful about his attempts to locate his sightings of Sidney Sweet.

"I'm sure once it was in front of the main post office," he said. "And a couple of times it was on North Meridian Street, but near The Circle. I really can't do much better than that."

Powder asked him to think further about it at his leisure. "OK," Kijovsky countered. "If you'll think about whether you're really fully insured." It was by way of a little joke.

Kijovsky turned his attention to constructing a picture with the police artist, and in half an hour a drawing was completed which Kijovsky stated was about as good as he could recall.

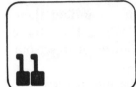**11** Powder drove back to Johnson's, his local grocery, before taking the artist's drawing and the three photographs obtained by Noble Perkins to Robert Sweet. But instead of shopping, Powder walked to the back of the store and knocked on an unmarked door between a bread rack and shelves of canned vegetables.

From inside he heard a grumbled sound which he took to be one of invitation. He opened the door and went in.

Uncle Adg, patriarch of a clan that extended far beyond its grocery center, sat facing the door. A vastly fat man, misnamed Agile by parents lacking the gift of prophecy, he ran the store and the family from a thronelike chair in the stock room. But family interests were broadly interpreted. Among other things, Johnson took an active part, by proxy, in the activities of the Lockerbie Residents Association, a civic organization of the old-guard "prerehabilitation" families, a shrinking number. Powder was a member.

"Mr. Powder," Uncle Adg said thoughtfully as his visitor entered. "Welcome. I haven't had the pleasure for some time now."

"I shop here regularly," Powder said.

"Ahh, that I know, that I know. Very grateful for your continued patronage, of course."

"I thought I'd take the opportunity to put in a request for some whole-meal pie dough."

Uncle Adg frowned. "We stock that, I think."

"But yours is made with animal fat."

"Ah," Uncle Adg said. "I'll look into it."

"Thank you."

The men knew that pie dough was not what Powder was there about.

"You're well, I hope," Powder said.

"Yes," Uncle Adg said, "and so, praise God, are my nearest and dearest."

"I'm pleased to hear that," Powder said.

"And your family, Mr. Powder?"

Powder shrugged. "My son is taking liberties with the conditions of his parole."

"I'm sorry to hear that," Uncle Adg said.

"My worry is that it indicates a frame of mind which will lead him back into antisocial activities."

Uncle Adg nodded slowly in agreement. "It does not bode well," he said.

"I would like," Powder said, "to ask a favor of you."

"And what would it be that I could do for you, Mr. Powder?" The fat man rubbed the sides of his mouth with the forefingers of both hands.

"I've been having a little trouble at my house," Powder said.

"Oh, yes?"

"I will be surprised if you haven't heard about my window."

Uncle Adg smiled broadly. "Now that you mention it . . ."

"A stone," Powder said, "and thrown during the day, which is not routine for vandalism."

"No," Uncle Adg agreed.

"And the previous day someone sprayed graffiti on the wall of my garage."

Uncle Adg frowned. "On the alley door?"

"No. On the side, where I go into my workshop. It's not plainly visible from either the alley or the street. Did you know about that?"

Uncle Adg thought for a moment before confessing, "No, I hadn't heard about the graffiti."

The two men were silent for a moment.

"Have you been home yet this evening, Mr. Powder?"

"No."

The two men repeated their silence.

"I see," Powder said.

"What exactly was it that you wanted me to do for you?" Uncle Adg asked.

"I thought that the next time you were out for a walk, if you happened to see someone behaving suspiciously in the immediate vicinity of my home, perhaps, if you had the time, you might follow him to see where he lived."

Powder knew Agile Johnson never stirred from the store. But he had "contacts," eyes and ears, all over the district.

"Such a thing might happen during my daily constitutional," Johnson said. "But, if I may ask a delicate question . . ."

"I am not seeking a prosecution," Powder said.

"I can see we are rapping on the same wavelength," Agile Johnson said slowly, clearly.

"Do you know who's responsible, Mr. Johnson?" Powder asked.

"No," the fat man said. "But I will keep my eyes open and see if I can be of service to you."

"I would be grateful."

Uncle Adg then nodded slowly. "You must come for a longer visit next time, Mr. Powder. A little beer. A bite to eat."

"All right," Powder said, conscious of the fact that the invitation to come back, equally with the implied suggestion of an immediate departure, was unusual. "That would be nice."

"Are you going home from here?"

"I hadn't planned to," Powder said. "But I think I will."

Powder drove the short distance from Johnson's to his house on Vermont Street. From the street he saw immediately a white swastika painted on his front door.

He got out of his car and walked up the path. The image was clear and evenly painted and it filled a panel in the lower half of the door.

Powder walked to his garage and found a can of brown paint. He carried it back to the front. Although the paint did not exactly match the color of the door, he painted the image out, leaving it visible only to someone standing near.

After replacing the paint and cleaning his brush, Powder returned to his car and drove to Bernard Avenue.

"These aren't my dad!" Robert Sweet said indignantly

"None of them? Look carefully."

"I ought to know what my own dad looks like," the boy said. He dropped the pictures of the three corpses and the police artist's drawing.

"That's true," Powder said. He rubbed his face. "Have you eaten yet?"

"Not exactly."

"You just go and nibble from time to time, is that right?" Robert Sweet shrugged.

"I'll cook if you wash the dishes," Powder said. "Fair?"

After a moment the boy said, "Fair."

"Do you follow the Indians?" Robert Sweet asked over a plate of lasagna.

"Not so much recently," Powder said. After a moment, "You ever hear of Ted Beard?"

Robert Sweet grinned. "Center fielder."

"Never quite made it with the White Sox, but we were always happy to have him back."

"We're the Expos' farm club now."

"I know," Powder said.

"Roger Maris played for us for one season in your day," Sweet said.

"And Rocky Colavito and Herb Score. You heard of Herb Score?"

"Nineteen fifty-six, when the Indians won the American Association pennant *and* beat the All Stars from the other teams in the league."

"I hadn't been married long, those days," Powder said. "Happy days."

"Are you married now?"

"No."

"Why do people stop being married?"

"I suppose it comes as a disappointment that not all years are nineteen fifty-sixes."

While Robert Sweet washed the dishes, Powder put Sidney Sweet's papers back in the desk and drawers he had taken them from.

Then, although he felt foolish doing it, he went around the father's bedroom examining walls and floors for hidden compartments.

He found nothing and he remained very uneasy about the lack of personal residues of the missing man.

"Hey," Robert Sweet said, "I did what you told me."

"What was that?"

"I bought something today." The boy hesitated. "With the money you gave me. You remember, don't you?"

"I remember."

"My dad will give it back to you when he gets home. I promise he will."

"Show me what you bought."

The boy smiled shyly, then brought an Indianapolis Indians autographed baseball bat from behind his back. He held it up, rotating it so Powder could see the printed signatures. Sweet smiled. "Some of the guys on the school team have them."

"Good," Powder said.

"Hey, Dad *will* pay you back. I know he will."

■ ■ ■

Powder left Robert Sweet shortly after eight o'clock. He stopped at the first bar he came to and carried a shot to a table next to a phone booth. He sat for a while. He thought of Ace Mencelli. He thought of Fleetwood, whom he hadn't seen again in the afternoon. He downed the drink. He went to the phone and dialed the number Mrs. Martha Miles— the first woman he ever took to bed—had given him earlier in the day.

"Roy!" she said. "I didn't expect to hear from you so soon."

"We might be dead tomorrow," Powder said. "So why waste time?"

Martha Miles asked him to give her until nine-thirty. He used the time to drive home again, shower and change his clothes, including clean underwear.

When she answered her door she looked fresh and clean. She whispered a greeting and pointed to a second door leading off the railed porch. "That's *his,*" she said. "The apartment is upstairs."

As if on cue they heard heavy steps. The second door opened and Powder moved back to allow a dark-haired man in his early twenties to step out. The young man had a rectangular face with a prominent chin, and he wore a droopy moustache that, perhaps, made him look a year or two older than he really was.

The man paused in front of Powder and Mrs. Miles, allowing the corners of his mouth to rise into a form of smile that was not supported by his eyes.

"Evening, Mrs. Miles," the young man said. He looked at one, then the other, and turned to pull his own door shut. He tested that it was securely closed and proceeded from the porch to the sidewalk, where he turned and walked away.

"He hardly ever goes out," Martha Miles said as the man

passed from sight. "I've only seen him half a dozen times in the last month. Maybe I'm just being stupid, but I'm scared to death of him."

"Painter you say his name is?"

"Henry Painter."

"Did he give you references when he took the place?"

She stepped back, feeling criticized. "He paid two months in advance."

"Has he actually done or said anything out of line?"

"No, no. But he's so, so . . . kind of arrogant." She shrugged and lifted her eyes to his. "A poor widow woman on her own. Not as young as she used to be. People like me get scared of things, I guess."

"Perhaps."

She invited him in.

As she closed the door she said, "The guy just gives me the creeps, Roy, he really does." She turned to face him. "Well," she said, "here we are."

Powder took her hands, which she gave quickly. He pulled her to him. He kissed her, roughly.

Later they went to Leonardo's, a nightclub on the Northeast, near the intersection of Post Road and Pendleton Pike. In the first part of the three hours they were there they talked much, if generally, about their life histories. Powder spoke emotionally about his broken marriage and about the much-loved house he left behind and about the son he also seemed to have lost with his divorce. Martha Miles, too, had had a son and once was married, though her husband was dead. He had died twenty-three years before.

"And you didn't get married again?"

Martha Miles looked at him wistfully. "Losing Joe was a terrible shock," she said. "Then later I put all my energy into bringing up little Terry. Marrying again just didn't happen. I had nothing against it, but I didn't go looking for it either. You know?"

"I know."

They were silent then, until Powder asked, "What have you done for money?"

A slight pain passed into her expression and she hesitated. "Ah, hell," Powder said. "Water under the bridge."

Rapidly he became loud and jolly. He called for much service and laughed a lot and plied Martha Miles with drink. He stopped asking her personal questions.

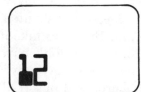 In his mail slot Friday morning Powder found a note saying that the fingerprints lifted off the glass, library book and razor from Sidney Sweet's house did not match any prints in the IPD files. Did Powder want, the note asked, a match request to be sent to the FBI?

Powder read the note and then stormed through the corridors to the Fingerprint Identification section.

Because it was half an hour before opening time, no one was there.

Nevertheless he rattled the doorknob vigorously and banged on the glass.

After a minute he stopped. On the back of the memo he wrote, "Why was I not called about this yesterday? Don't you guys realize that putting things in mail slots can cost lives?"

He slid the memo under the door and walked, humming, to the Missing Persons office.

"You look pleased with yourself," Fleetwood said as he entered.

"It's a brave face. I'm confused and hemmed in by things I don't understand."

Fleetwood became concerned. "Is there anything I can do, Leroy?"

Powder considered and was about to speak when the office door opened. Sue Swatts entered and, beaming, said, "Morning, everyone. A beautiful day, isn't it?"

Powder turned on her, suddenly furious. He said, "What makes you so goddamned sickeningly sweet and happy all the time, Swatts? I want you to stop it. Have moods. Be nasty. Get angry. Become a human being, for a change."

Officer Swatts, usually up to Powder's sudden rages, was caught off guard this time and went rigid. The color drained from her face.

Fleetwood saw this immediately and became angry. "You're an emotional cripple, Powder," Fleetwood shouted. "You get annoyed with your own life and then you take it out on whoever else happens to be handy. You don't have the right to do that, not to Sue, not to me, not to anybody."

"Susan," Powder said immediately, "Carollee, I'm sorry."

The apology surprised them as much as his outburst had.

Twenty minutes later, at two minutes past nine, Powder's internal telephone rang. Expecting it to be Fingerprints, he answered harshly.

"My, my, who got out of the wrong side of the wrong bed this morning?" Tidmarsh asked.

"Oh. It's you," Powder said rather stupidly.

"Thought you might pop up when you get a chance. I promise not to make any loud noises if hangover is one of your problems."

A minute later the telephone rang again.

"What now?" Powder asked.

"Look, Powder, it was *you* who asked *me* about a regular missing-persons slot on CCC's cable channel," Lieutenant Miller said. "If you don't want to take it any further, that's all right by me."

Two minutes later the telephone rang a third time. Finally

wiser, Powder took a breath before picking up the receiver. He answered politely.

A high nasal voice said, "This is Sappolino of the Fingerprint Identification Department. We have received your message, but I would like to point out on behalf of my colleagues and myself that there are recognized and established procedures for urgent fingerprint identification searches. The procedure, for future reference, is that you mark your identification request 'urgent,' in red ink and in a prominent position. Moreover, your current wishes as to our question about a further search with the FBI are still not clear. Can you tell me whether you want the impressions forwarded and if so whose budget it should go on? Also whether you wish it to be categorized as urgent."

It was another fifteen minutes before the disposition of the day's routine work was completed to Powder's satisfaction. Swatts reported that the Night Cover team had recorded two unidentified bodies overnight and she left the office to acquire details, photographs and fingerprints. Haddix asked to speak to Powder for a few minutes about the care of the missing father of the bride-to-be, but the conversation only amounted to a report that the father had not yet been located. Fleetwood settled to some paper work, after having been out of the office so much the previous day.

Noble Perkins gave Powder a copy of the past year's statements from Sidney Sweet's bank account. In exchange Powder gave him two more names to draw files for: Henry Painter, Martha Miles.

When Perkins was tucked up in his corner, Powder sat down next to Fleetwood at her desk. "We're going to have to stop meeting like this," he said.

"Why?" Fleetwood asked.

"Hey, got a question for you. Answer it for me and you get me out of a hole."

Fleetwood said nothing.

"Got this guy, moves to a house that somebody else buys pretending to be him, and then he—"

"Hey, hang on! Somebody else—"

"You heard, but that's not what I want to ask you about," Powder said. "Then this guy gets a job where he draws more money than he works for."

"He—?"

"You're an impatient broad, aren't you?" Powder said. "*Then* the guy gets married and has a kid, but ten or eleven years later the wife suddenly skips off. *Then* a year and a half later the guy skips off himself, leaving the kid, and without warning."

"What do you mean that—"

"Hang on, hang on. I'm only getting my breath. Now the bit I want to ask you about is this: The guy doesn't let people take pictures of him, and—this is the goddamn thing that bugs me most—he doesn't have any personal items around the house. No letters, no dog tag, no report cards, no second-place medals for swimming races, no gilded baby boots, no nothing. No pictures of his grandmother or his first car. Not even vacation slides. *Everybody* has vacation slides, don't they?"

"Maybe his wife took them with her."

"Maybe," Powder said.

"Have you talked to her?"

"She's supposed to be in Mexico," Powder said. But he was thoughtful.

"I don't know, Powder." Fleetwood shrugged.

"You're a lot of good, aren't you?"

"I was going to ask, before . . ."

"What?"

"What do you mean someone pretends to be him to buy his house?"

Powder spread his hands. "That's what what I got seems to mean."

"What do you mean the guy draws more money than he works for?"

"That's what his records show."

"Anything where somebody is getting money for nothing sounds fishy to me," Fleetwood said. "The guy must be some kind of a crook or a spy or *something!*"

Powder looked at her with a kind of admiration. "That's what I always said about you, Fleetwood. You really got your feet on the ground."

Tidmarsh looked tired.

"You look tired," Powder said.

Tidmarsh laughed. "To think a wreck like you has the nerve to say something like that to me . . ." He shook his head.

Powder sat silently.

"OK," Tidmarsh said. "I thought you would like to know that I found a kind of flaw in Mencelli's work this morning."

"This morning?" Powder asked. He looked at his watch.

"Well, I have trouble sleeping sometimes," Tidmarsh said. "And it's quiet around here early on."

"I spent a lifetime working at night," Powder said. "I know about the A.M peace."

"Ah, yes," Tidmarsh said, remembering that Powder spent years in charge of Night Cover. Then, "You know, your friend Mencelli is a genuinely devious character."

"You make it sound like a compliment."

"I checked some of his source numbers, just a few. And he's worked out some impressive techniques to get into the out-of-state data banks he drew on. He certainly gets an A-plus for hacking."

"But you say there's a flaw?"

"It has to do with the way the periods of comparison are defined. Mencelli's argument is that more people in certain categories died than would be expected. But to say that, you must choose what numbers you compare to what and that determines how many you would expect to die."

"Oh," Powder said.

"I think that he has picked the comparisons that maximize the effect he thinks he's found rather than what might, objectively, be considered the best comparisons."

Powder looked thoughtful.

"He hasn't done anything wrong," Tidmarsh said, "but it is possible to do it differently and that way you can reduce the chances of the effect really being there. You can get the statistical significance down from over ninety-nine percent to a little better than sixty-seven percent."

"So it's still better than even that something's happening."

"Ah," Tidmarsh said, "in one sense, yes, but in a statistical sense it means that it could well be insignificant."

"Reinterpreted the way you've done it."

"Yes."

"Is there any reason to say one interpretation is more right than the other?"

"No," Tidmarsh said definitely. "But if our guideline is that we have to be as sure as we can be, then we are a lot less sure now than we were before."

"Even though more people in those categories have died recently in Indiana than in the other states."

"It may just be chance. That's what we're talking about, Powder. You *could* flip a coin and get heads seven times in a row, but that doesn't mean the coin has two heads. A thousand heads in a row isn't a guarantee either, but it is much better evidence."

Powder took a deep breath and rubbed his face with both hands. "Do you know how long this thing has been going on, if it's going on?" Powder asked.

"The effect, if it exists, began about seven years ago," Tidmarsh said.

"And did you ever work on how many people it would have had to involve?"

"About twenty-six hundred."

Powder's eyebrows went up. "Twenty-six hundred people died who wouldn't have been expected to and you still don't know whether there was an 'effect' or not?"

Tidmarsh smiled patiently. "Two thousand six hundred, plus or minus nearly two thousand. Spread over seven years. It could be less than a hundred a year. And those divided between several categories."

"But there could be"—Powder calculated—"there could be six hundred and fifty people a year for seven years."

"Yes."

Powder rubbed his face. "Two full jumbo jets a year for seven years."

"Statistics is a blunt tool, Powder. It may just be the luck of the draw."

"You say there are two ways to approach whether it all exists or not."

"Two at the extremes. There would be other ways that would give answers in between."

Powder rose from his chair and approached Tidmarsh's desk. "You're a cop," he said. "And not a bad one."

"Thanks very much."

"I want to talk to you as a cop now, and not as a glorified adding machine. I want your gut feeling on this, Tidmarsh. Which way do you go?"

Tidmarsh shook his head. "I can't play like that, Powder. All I know for sure is that the evidence so far indicates we should do more work on it all."

Powder returned to his chair. He sat. He exhaled heavily. "Are you going to do more work on it?"

"Ah," Tidmarsh said. "That's another problem."

"Is it now?"

"I've thought it through as carefully as I can, but I cannot see any way that I could let Mencelli use our computers. It's not *just* the security problems and the data that he shouldn't have access to under any circumstances. I can't even see any practical way I could give him the required computer time without it being found out."

"Even if *he* worked through the night."

Tidmarsh spread his hands. "I just don't think it can be done."

 Powder walked thoughtfully down the stairs to the first floor.

When he entered the Missing Persons office, Howard Haddix was talking intently to Sue Swatts at the counter. Fleetwood worked at her desk.

"Got a lead on that eighteen-year father, Howard?" Powder asked.

Haddix looked up, puzzled. Then he shook his head slowly and said, "No, no. I've just been telling Sue I had a real bad attack from my shortness of breath again, since last night."

"Shouldn't have washed it on such a high temperature," Powder said.

"Excuse me?"

"Your breath," Powder said.

"I . . ."

"Don't mind him, Howie," Swatts said quietly.

"Hey, Susan! You're learning!" Powder said heartily. He approached and pounded her on the back. "Good old Swatts." He looked at his watch. "Picked up the leaflets from Printing yet?"

"I was just going."

"OK," Powder said, nodding. "You take it easy now."

"I will," Swatts said. "I will. You want to come along, Howie?"

"Sure."

Walking slowly, at Haddix's pace, they left the office.

Fleetwood said sharply, "Powder, why can't you just take the good things they have to offer without hassling them about the rest?"

Powder shrugged.

"Are you suddenly in a good mood?"

He considered the question. "I don't think so," he said. "But I'd like to talk to you about some things."

"All right."

"Do you have any free minutes tonight?"

She thought. "I can manage that," she said. Then she asked, "Have you done anything about that money you're getting?"

"No."

"It's naughty not to write a thank-you note."

His hands rose to his eyes and then followed his forehead all the way back to where they found some hair. "You're not angling for a meal, are you?"

Fleetwood said, "You may not be interested, but used right, somebody could do good things with that kind of cash."

"I've already seen a guy about investing in this great little vineyard in New Mexico."

"New Mexico?"

A woman, walking uncertainly, entered the office.

"Uh oh," Powder said. "Another husband absconded with a teenage tootsie."

"I have it on the highest authority that in this office we never get flippant about other people's troubles."

"I stand corrected," Powder said.

"Besides, isn't it more likely to be yet another one of your old flames looking to be rekindled?"

■ ■ ■

Powder sat down next to Noble Perkins. "How you doing, son?"

"On your list, you mean?"

"Sure do."

"Come on, Lieutenant. It's hard sometimes to fit in the work that you want with the department routine I'm supposed to do. The forms and all that."

"I thought you'd have built yourself a little robot to work through the boring stuff."

"Give me some of that money you don't seem to want and I will," Perkins said intently.

Powder was surprised that Perkins had paid enough attention to know about the inheritance. But he carried on, saying, "I know, Noble. I know. You're doing a grand job."

"All I've done is put the names through the data bank."

"What's it turned up?"

"The woman, Miles, has some minor offenses and two accessory-to-fraud convictions." He found a page of printout. "There are two Henry Painters on file, Senior and Junior. Senior has a long record, but he's dead. I didn't print it. Thought I'd ask which was the one you wanted."

Fingering Martha Miles's arrest record, Powder said, distantly, "Might as well pull the basics on both."

"OK."

"I shall return," Powder said. He folded the computer printout and put it in a pocket.

Imelda Nason remembered him. But the memory was not, from the expression on her face, one of pleasure. "You think you can just come around here anytime and talk to Earle?" she asked. "He's a busy guy. He needs his peace and quiet."

"It's you I would like to talk to, Mrs. Nason."

"What about?" Sharply.

"May I come in?"

She considered it for what felt a long time. Then she said, "Hang on."

After a good minute she came back. "He says to invite you in."

She held tight to the door as he went by.

Earle Nason's rocky figure filled a comfortable armchair in the couple's living room. He sat with a magazine, in slippers. He wore a satin bathrobe with a curlicued *EN* monogram. "Our friend in blue," he said affably. "You found my brother-in-law yet?"

"Not yet, Mr. Nason."

"Gee, that's too bad." He put the magazine on his lap. "Pull up a hay bale."

Powder sat. Mrs. Nason remained standing.

"Mel says it's her you want to talk to. You want me to leave the room?" He looked an immovable object.

"Nope," Powder said.

"So what do you want?" Imelda Nason asked.

"Do you know where your sister is, Mrs. Nason?"

Imelda Nason glanced at her husband. Then she said, "No. I said before. Don't you remember?"

"I remember," Powder said amiably. "But you struck me as the type of person who valued family above all things."

"My family ain't shit," she said.

"Still, you might have heard from her."

"Well," Mrs. Nason said uneasily, "since she left him, maybe. But I don't know where she is now. I haven't had nothing from her for a long time."

"How long?"

"I don't know exactly."

"Where was she when you heard from her last?"

Again she looked at her husband. Nason said, "Go on. Help the guy. He's just doing his job."

"Guadalajara."

"That's somewhere in the West of Mexico, isn't it?"

"I guess."

"Who is she with?"

"I don't know."

"I mean who was she with? When she ran away."

"Go on," Nason urged.

"This guy called Dolf Manan."

"What sort of business is he in?"

"Look," Imelda Nason said angrily, "what the hell is all this about? Why suddenly all the questions about Sunny and who she's with and where she is?"

"I am trying to find her husband, or ex-husband."

"What's it to do with her?"

"She might know where Sweet would have gone, better than the child does."

"Yeah? Well she doesn't. She wouldn't. They wasn't getting on very good for a long time."

"Why was that?"

"He was always a funny guy. Always. Edgy."

"Oh, yes?"

"Always fussing around. He'd go out to get the newspaper and he'd lock the door behind him, you know? Sunny thought it was kind of cute at first. You know, when the guy was a bit lively. But by the time she took off she didn't have anything to do with him. She was just waiting for the chance to go."

"Despite the child?"

"Well, the chance didn't really include the kid, you know what I mean?"

"And this Manan?"

Imelda Nason shrugged. "Kind of a small-time operator, with a few connections in Mexico. I suppose she's comfortable enough. The guy's a few laughs at least."

Powder nodded, then turned to Earle Nason. "You said that you last saw Sweet in Leonardo's."

Nason raised an eyebrow. "That's right. Like I saw you last night."

"If Sweet wasn't much on good times, what was he doing there?"

"Tell you the truth, I think maybe he was looking around for Sunny."

"Did your sister-in-law spend time at Leonardo's?"

"Some."

"Is that where she met Dolf Manan?"

"Coulda been. I don't really know."

"But she hung out there?"

"I seen all kinds of people at Leonardo's. It's a classy place. We've had senators there, and judges. That's the way the boss likes it."

Powder nodded. "I would still like to find Mrs. Sweet," he said. "Even if she doesn't know where her husband is now, she still might have things that would help me."

"Like what?" Mrs. Nason asked.

"She might know where his parents lived."

"They were dead."

"Or other relatives?"

"He didn't have any."

"Or she might have a picture of him. There aren't any at his house."

"*I've* got a picture of him."

Powder's face expressed surprise. "If I could borrow it, I would be very grateful."

Mrs. Nason chewed the inside of a cheek. She looked at her husband. He nodded. She left the room.

Earle Nason said lightly, "Don't mind Mel. She's had a pretty rough ride, one time and another, from guys like you. So she don't feel, you know, helpful right away when you come asking questions."

"We are a pretty nosy bunch of people," Powder said.

Nason laughed. "Yeah. Sticking all kinds of nose into other people's business."

"Yeah," Powder said in a comradely way, "and putting all kinds of stuff together which is really just coincidence."

Still laughing, Nason said, "Suspicious bastards, cops. Not that I've had much to do with them since my little bit of trouble."

"Funny you should mention your little bit of trouble," Powder said, smiling.

"What you mean?" Nason asked easily.

"A good example of a guy like me taking things and drawing conclusions."

Nason's good humor went into a rapid decline.

"What I mean," Powder continued, "is how the man you killed without intending to just happened to be the brother of the man you work for now. The same brother that took over all the dead man's business operations."

Nason's expression lost all vestige of friendliness, but before he spoke again Imelda Nason returned to the room. She carried four photographs.

She handed them to Powder. "These were from their wedding."

Powder rose. "I was just saying to your husband what a very nice house you have here. Good bit of land with it, and very comfortable inside. You must be very pleased he has such a well-paid job."

"We do OK," Imelda Nason said. "But it hasn't always been like this."

"That's just what I was saying." Powder held the pictures up and said, "I'll take good care of them and I'll get them back to you soon. Thanks very much for your help."

Powder moved to depart and Mrs. Nason seemed surprised that he had suddenly decided to leave.

"Make sure the son of a bitch goes out the door," Earle Nason said angrily to his wife.

Powder quickly pulled away from the Nasons' house, but at the end of the street he turned. After circling the block, he parked where he could see the Nasons' driveway.

Then he had a look at the photographs.

Powder recognized only Imelda Nason among the nine people in the photographs. But of course, Earle would still have been in prison then.

Even at his wedding Sidney Sweet had done his best to avoid a clear picture. But in one, Powder finally had a good look at the face of the man he was trying to find. Not by any stretch of the imagination a big man; sandy-haired, bright-eyed, wiry.

Mrs. Nason's sister, Sunny, was a small blond woman who looked appropriately radiant on her wedding day, and very young.

An older couple might have been somebody's parents. Two other men and a woman Powder had no ideas about.

The ninth person, another man, looked rather like a basketball player gone to seed.

Powder had been parked for fifteen of the thirty minutes he had allowed himself when Earle Nason left his house, now wearing a business suit and tie.

Nason drove off quickly in a black Buick, and Powder almost lost him at first. But later, when they joined Massachusetts Avenue at 38th Street, Nason suddenly slowed down. He took a left on Kercheval, did the horseshoe and turned back onto Massachusetts, heading toward the city again.

At Layman Avenue he went left, then pulled up and stopped.

Powder drew in behind him.

Nason got out of the car and walked back to Powder's window. Powder leaned out. "Lost your way? Mass Av runs straight into Pendleton Pike."

"What the fuck do you want, cop?"

"Nothing you haven't already made clear to me," Powder said. He revved his motor, backed up and squealed away past the angry bodyguard.

On his way back to police headquarters, Powder stopped at the insurance office of Morris Kijovsky.

"Hey, Lieutenant!" Kijovsky said after Powder was led to his desk by a receptionist. "You're lucky to find me in." Kijovsky walked around to him, shook hands. "Found that missing man yet?"

"No," Powder said, "but I'd like to show you some pictures."

"Pictures? Sure. I like pictures." Kijovsky dropped onto the edge of his desk. Powder passed him Sweet's wedding photographs.

"Hey, nice body on the bride," Kijovsky said.

"Do you recognize anyone?"

Kijovsky handed them back. "Sure. That's this guy Sweet."

"Show me."

Kijovsky pointed immediately to the basketball player.

After parking in the Department lot, Powder went straight to the Photography Section. There he arranged for many enlarged copies of Sidney Sweet's face and a few of the basketball player.

"The phone's been buzzing for you, Powder." Fleetwood waved some message memos at him.

"Anything interesting?"

"Well, your girl friend sounded pretty eager to have you call her back."

Powder stared at Fleetwood for a moment. The he burst

into enthusiasm. "Yeah? Really? What'd she say? Gosh. Whizz. Where's my phone!"

Fleetwood raised her eyes momentarily, an optical sigh. She handed him the messages.

Powder looked down at her. He kicked at a tire. "When the hell are you going to get out of that wheelbarrow?"

Martha Miles *was* clearly pleased to speak to him. "It wasn't urgent or anything, Leroy," she said. "I hope I'm not interrupting something important."

"No," Powder said.

"I wanted to thank you for last night. I wanted to say that I had a lovely time, that it's been a long time since I went out and enjoyed myself so much. Or enjoyed myself at all. And, well, I'm grateful."

Powder looked up and saw Fleetwood watching him, smiling slightly.

Staring back at Fleetwood, he said, "I had a great time too, Martha. I hope we can do it again sometime soon."

"That would please me a lot," Martha Miles said.

"In a day or two?"

"Oh, good."

"I'll call you."

"I'll be waiting."

"OK. Bye now."

"Bye."

When Powder hung up, Fleetwood asked, "Hey, Powder, what was she like? I mean back then. Originally."

"Terrible," Powder said. "She's a whole lot better now."

Powder sat next to Noble Perkins as the young man worked at his desk. "Nobe, old buddy?"

Perkins didn't respond immediately.

"Nobe, I want to know about your love life."

"What?" Perkins didn't move his head, but showed that he had heard by turning red.

"You've been working here ... how long now? Nine months?"

"A year next week, Lieutenant."

"You got a girl, Nobe?"

"Aw, come on, Lieutenant!"

"Or maybe a couple?"

"Cut it out, Lieutenant!" Perkins was smiling, redly.

"It's just I was thinking. There was a little girl who worked in here a couple years ago. Great little kid, called Agnes. She got herself moved into our computer section and has a police scholarship to finish college. What say I arrange to introduce the two of you? I figure you got a lot of things in common."

"Aw, Lieutenant," Perkins said, "stop your joshing me now, hey!"

Powder stopped joshing. He wrote out another name to get police records on: Joseph Miles, Martha Miles's late husband. They had married a couple of years after Martha had last seen Powder, following the completion of their brief and unglamorous period of intimacy. Joseph Miles had died eight years later. But he had been named with her on both her convictions.

In exchange, Perkins handed Powder the police records on the Henry Painters and the Husk brothers, Arnold and "Mister Jimmy." As he did so, he asked, "This new name, Lieutenant. What do you want?"

"Whatever we have on file. Nothing fancy. Yet."

Powder looked at the other telephone messages. Two were internal, from Fingerprints and from Captain Graniela's office. Another was from Mr. Cass Beehler, asking what Powder had found out about his daughter, Jacqueline.

Powder laid the three phone memos on his desk top. He reread them. The he covered them with the printout on the Painters.

Painter Senior had been dead fifteen years, his life of

crime having been cut short, at age forty-eight, by a small-caliber pistol fired into his brain from the top of the back of his neck.

The murder was unsolved. The body had been found in the Grand Calumet River Lagoon near Gary, Indiana. Painter had lived and operated in Gary and was considered, in the records, to be the Gary representative of a loosely organized area criminal consortium based in Chicago. Gary, with Hammond and East Chicago, were the Indiana end of the Greater Chicago strip of cities along the southwestern shores of Lake Michigan.

Painter's son, Henry Junior, was listed as seven and in grade school at the time of the killing.

Painter Junior had gone on to complete high school and had been fined twice, following two relatively minor drug convictions the year after. He was now twenty-two. The address on the records was his mother's Gary address. No employment was listed.

Junior was the only son, although Painter Senior had had two daughters by a previous wife in the early fifties. Both older sisters were married and neither lived in Indiana. There was no detail about the disposition of the first wife. The second wife had never been suspected of criminal activity. There was no indication of what she had done since her husband's death.

Painter Senior's known and suspected activities were broadly based and traditional for a man who was something of a gangland boss, even if in a relatively small area. He had spent more than twelve of his forty-eight years in jail, though none in the decade before his murder.

Powder folded the documents when he had finished reading them a second time. The action revealed the telephone memos.

He rang Fingerprints.

"Oh, yeah, Powder," the nasal voice of Sappolino said. "It's about those prints we sent to the FBI."

"I didn't think it was about the tread on my left front tire," Powder said.

"What?"

Powder waited.

"We've had two funny calls from the Feds about your print request," the voice said, seeming to try to begin again.

"Oh, yes?"

"The first one was some kind of routine asking what security clearance we had."

Despite himself, Powder repeated, "Security clearance?"

"You know what that's about?"

"Negative."

"Then we got this other call that said they had no records that matched the prints anyway."

Powder considered.

"Are you there, Lieutenant Powder?"

"Do you usually get phone calls when prints aren't on record?"

"No. The message comes on the telex thing."

"Have you ever had calls before?"

"Not that I can remember. But I wouldn't want to say never."

"All right. Thanks."

"So what you want us to do with them now?"

"Send them in again. Say they're double urgent."

"Do I put it—"

"Yes, on my budget," Powder said.

Then he called Graniela's office.

"The captain's not available at the moment, Lieutenant Powder," a receptionist said.

"I've got this message to call him immediately."

"That's right. I know he wants to see you."

"When, then?"

"Can you come up in about fifteen minutes?"

"I suppose."

"All right. We'll see you then."

"What's it all about?" Powder asked.

"I don't know exactly. But it's something about reducing the size of the Missing Persons Department. Does that make any sense to you?"

Powder refused to sit as he waited for Captain Graniela. For ten minutes he paced, scowling and muttering.

When Graniela buzzed, the receptionist, relieved, jumped up and ushered Powder through.

Graniela, in a brown sweat suit, looked even more like a bear than usual. Barbells on the floor and a stopwatch in his hand made it clear that Powder had been kept waiting so Graniela could complete a fitness routine. "I like to keep a bit of tone," the captain said as he wrote on a clipboard, "now I'm more on the administrative side of things."

"Some of us have to spend our days doing police work," Powder said acidly.

"When we have enough to do to justify our existence," Graniela replied sharply, though he was still looking down. The man had a reputation for hard, unimaginative thinking. He picked up a towel and sat. He wiped at his face and arms.

"What's that supposed to mean?"

"How is the Missing Persons throughput holding up?"

"Higher than ever."

"Mmmm. That *is* what I read in these general circulation memos you keep sending around."

Powder sat.

"And your solution rate?"

"We call it a resolution rate and it's the best in the Midwest."

"Mmmm."

Powder sat.

"Still leaves you a lot of time to work on non-Missing Persons cases," Graniela said.

"What?"

Graniela leaned forward. "Are you deaf, Lieutenant?"

"I find nonsense harder to hear than sense," Powder said.

Graniela leaned back in his chair. "Nonsense, huh?" He looked at his fitness clipboard. He made another note on it. "Nonsense?" He snorted.

Powder waited.

"I was in the field as a detective for a long time, Powder. A damn sight longer than you ever were. I have a lot of contacts, both outside the force and inside it."

Powder looked at his watch.

"I hear things."

"Like what?"

"Like I hear you've been making a lot of requests for police records on people who, when I have them cross-checked against your own section's file index, don't seem to be mentioned in Missing Persons reports. I ask myself why. So I ask you, why?"

"Because," Powder said icily, "I bust my gut tracking down shadows and suspicions and it's the kind of attitude that differentiates our resolution rate from departments where they don't try so hard."

"But names not mentioned in MP reports?" Graniela asked again pointedly. "I'd have thought anything—even 'shadows'—worth pulling files on ought to be mentioned in your reports. So, from here it looks either like gross inefficiency, or . . ."

"Or what?"

"If they're not MP names, then they must be something else. *Could* be they are even *for* someone else. *Could* be you're selling the information we have here to somebody outside."

"I'm corrupt, now, am I?" Powder asked, the tone of his voice rising sharply. "That's why I spend all my winters in

Florida and my summers in Europe instead of working away
all my waking hours?" Powder shook his head in furious dis-
gust. "You ask me these absurd questions. I got to ask myself
a question. I ask myself why? So I ask you, why are you
hassling me, Graniela?"

"Hassle? I don't hassle. But we got a lot of pressure on cost
these days. We got to look at all this kind of thing. So, I ask
you again, why are you pulling records that aren't on your
Missing Person reports?"

"We come across things in the section that may need investigating."

" 'Investigating' is it now? 'Things?' " Graniela rocked
forward. "So why not pass these 'things' on to the people
whose job it is to do the investigating around here? Why are
you doing it yourself, if you're so goddamned busy with
missing goddamned persons down there?"

Powder said nothing.

"If you got time to do detective work while you're in MP,
then there's too much slack in MP. You see what I'm saying?"

"I'll match my department's record against anybody's."

"Well, you might just have to do that," Graniela said de-
finitively.

Powder said nothing.

"Besides, that's not all I hear. I get this whisper that you're
cooking something up with Tidmarsh. What's that about?"

"We're both into health food, so we trade recipes over
lunch," Powder said.

"Oh, that's nice," Graniela said, with overplayed sarcasm.
"What kind of stuff? Nut cutlets?"

"Yeah, and bulgur wheat salads and tofu and mung beans
and brown rice juice."

"So why is Tidmarsh suddenly coming to work at night?"

"Gee, Captain, I don't know. You better ask him. But I've
spent a lifetime coming in out of hours and nobody ever
complained to me. So before you go crazy you might con-

sider whether pushing him about it might not be counter-
productive. On a cost-effectiveness basis."

"*And* I hear from Special Investigations you're off on some
flier about a . . ." Graniela searched on his desk. Special Investigations was the department that dealt with inquiries
concerning prominent people.

Graniela found a piece of paper and studied it. "About a
James Husk," he said. "What's that about?"

Powder looked at him. "Special Investigations, huh?"
Powder's eyes narrowed; he pointed a finger. "I have this
ugly, stinking feeling that we've finally got around to what
all this crap is really about."

Graniela, who thought he had been subtle, hesitated for a
moment.

"Mister Jimmy has some clout, it would seem," Powder
said.

"What's your interest, Powder?"

"I've never met the man," Powder said lightly, "though in
the course of the normal pursuance of work on a Missing
Persons case I have come across the guy who put him where
he is."

"Why are you pulling files on him?"

"I am thorough by nature."

"Special Investigations don't want you meddling."

"Then we understand each other," Powder said.

"Do we?"

"Because I don't want them meddling either." Powder
stood up. "Just pass the message on, will you, errand boy? If
they've got work that I might foul up, then tell them to talk
directly to me in simple English. But if it's just that they're
answerable to Mister Jimmy and he's told them to take the
pressure off the guy who killed his brother, then somebody
better explain the concept of 'counterproductivity' to them
too." Powder waved his finger at Graniela. "Suddenly this
whole thing has the pure odor of a scare-off. I *can* be scared
off things, but not by the likes of you."

"I've supported the increase in the Missing Persons budget in the past, Powder," Graniela said, breathing heavily. "In fact, I think it's fair to say that I was a vital factor in getting your section expanded to where it is now."

"Which means you are capble of responding to reasonable arguments, clearly stated. That is a good quality for someone in your position."

"Which means," Graniela shouted, breaking from his shaky self-control, "that I can take my support away and make your life a whole lot less comfortable than it is now. All those pussy-licking newspaper articles about reunited families when some asshole strolls back through the same door he strolled out of, no thanks to you. They make me sick. Call that PR crap police work? My granny could do what you do, Powder, and she's been dead for twenty-five years."

"Well, you dig her up and roll her in. We've got so much work, we need all the help we can get."

Powder arrived at the table just as Tidmarsh was spreading his napkin on his lap.

"Ah, my luncheon cabaret," Tidmarsh said.

"I've just been told we're hatching something up together."

"Oh, yes? What? A chicken?" Tidmarsh looked at Powder, sought humorous response, found none, tried again. "A goose?"

"I've been up with Graniela," Powder said.

"Society's beachhead for the 'new realism' in police procedures. What did he want? Blackjack practice?"

"You've met the man," Powder observed.

"Since I took my new role, as acting head, we've had one or two conjunctions."

"Well, he's just told me that I have been drawing arrest records on people not mentioned in my Missing Persons reports."

"I see," Tidmarsh said.

"Did he order the cross-check through you?"

"No, as a matter of fact, he didn't."

"He also told me that you've been coming in at night."

"Did he now?"

"So he has a direct line to someone in your department. I think the work on me was done this morning, late in the morning. Does that timing suggest anybody in particular to you?"

Tidmarsh ruminated. "It might," he said. "I'll run through my own records this afternoon."

"So at least now you know," Powder said. He rose.

"No lunch?"

"I'm dining elsewhere today," Powder said. "Hey, did you pass the good news on to Jules Mencelli yet?"

"I called him this morning."

"And did he like it?"

"I think it's fair to say he wasn't pleased. As much as anything he is upset that he's not going to get computer time here."

"Awww. Poor baby."

"He also thinks I don't know my bit from my byte."

"Sweet guy," Powder said.

"I asked him to come in this afternoon. He's going to give me a lesson in computer analysis."

In a luncheonette called Mary's, five blocks from the City-County Building, Powder found a man and woman deep in cheerful conversation. The man was Lieutenant Miller, and as soon as he noticed Powder approaching he stood up. He adopted a formal demeanor. He said, "You're late."

"I've been helping Captain Graniela with his priorities."

"Oh," Miller said. Then, "This is Ms. Wendy Winslow of the CCC Television Network. Champaign Cable Company."

"How do you do, Ms. Winslow?"

Wendy Winslow, bright and friendly, stood and shook Powder's proffered hand enthusiastically.

They all sat again and immediately a bony waiter came to the table and addressed Powder. "I am seeing your threesome is complete. Would you be wishing to order now, sir? Your colleagues have already made their choosings clear to me but they were waiting their service for your arrival."

"Do you have anything in the way of a nut cutlet?" Powder asked.

The waiter plucked a kiss from his mouth and said, "Our nut cutlets will be making you forget any other nut cutlet you have ever tasted."

"With whatever it should go with," Powder said.

The waiter bowed, silently accepting the responsibility. He retreated.

"Are you vegetarian, Lieutenant?" Wendy Winslow asked.

"No," Powder said.

Miller explained, "Lieutenant Powder has a reputation for eccentricity."

"Lieutenant Miller is saying I'm a nut case, Ms. Winslow," Powder said.

Winslow smiled brightly. "Good. Let's talk about your idea."

"I figure," Powder said, "a program focused on missing people could help you and could help us. It's got human interest; it's got drama; it's got mystery. It's also topical, with the extra attention missing people have been getting lately. But the special element we can offer is a potential personality, actually from within the section."

"Would that be you?"

"Certainly not. You remember a few years ago, the police-woman who was shot and paralyzed waist-down following a stakeout of some armed robbers?"

"I'm not sure I do," Winslow said.

"Gorgeous woman to look at, articulate and tough, good brain. The media all picked her up at the time. She even had a TV news offer, but she turned it down to stay on the force. On the other hand, our enlightened police brass was reluctant to let her back on active duty—you know, the paralysis—but after all the media pressure they caved in and compromised by putting her in Missing Persons."

"I see," Winslow said. She glanced at Miller, whose steady return gaze effectively confirmed Powder's account.

"At this point Missing Persons would fall apart without her. When I retire, which might not be very long from now, she's a shoo-in to make lieutenant and be put in charge. But she's not that everything-mapped-out kind of person. She thrives on challenges. So what I was thinking was this—a widely advertised pilot, then a spot every week for a while. If that went all right, ultimately a spot on the news every day, like the weather." Powder looked earnestly at Winslow. "It could be a real puller for you," he said. "And the point is, this little gal is genuinely right in the middle of it." Powder sat back, finished.

Wendy Winslow nodded slowly. "It sounds intriguing, but have you ever actually watched CCC's cable output in Indianapolis?"

Fleetwood was out when Powder returned to the office. There was nothing in the log and neither Swatts nor Haddix remembered her saying where she was going.

Not bothering to ask Noble Perkins, Powder sat at his desk for a while and ruminated.

Finally he settled to work and pulled out the file of outstanding case reports he considered as candidates for inclusion in the next "Have You Seen Them?" sheet.

Almost as a reward for good behavior, Fleetwood rolled in through the office door.

She looked worried.

Powder watched thoughtfully as she made her way to her desk. She dropped her purse on it, pushed a few papers around, then leaned back, still.

Powder rolled his swivel chair along a path between desks to sit beside her. "Speaking cripple to cripple," he said, "you look upset."

Fleetwood did not respond at first.

Gently he asked, "Come on, what's up, kid?"

She looked at him. "You won't like it. You won't think it's anything."

"Two for the price of one. How can I lose?"

"Jules is not at home," Fleetwood said.

Powder waited. There was no amplification. "That's it?"

"That's it. I went over at lunchtime and he wasn't there."

"Was he expecting you?"

"Not exactly. It wasn't stated."

"But it was understood."

"Yes." She seemed to think. She nodded. "Yes."

"Does he have a car?"

"Yes. It wasn't there."

"So . . . ?"

"So sure, maybe he went somewhere. But it *feels* wrong to me."

"He's probably just come in to see Tidmarsh."

She looked at him. "What about?"

"Tidmarsh thinks there is reason to doubt the statistical significance of Mencelli's conclusion. Tidmarsh called him this morning and Ace was supposed to come in this afternoon to talk it over."

"I see," Fleetwood said. She thought about it.

Powder watched her for a while. He reached back to his telephone and called Tidmarsh. But Jules Mencelli had not yet come to see him.

"Let me know when he does appear, will you?"

"OK," Tidmarsh said.

Powder dialed Jules Mencelli's home number. There was no answer.

"So where's he gone?" Fleetwood asked.

"He's your friend. You want to ask around, go do it."

Powder worked through a pile of paper. He also considered whether he could open Jules Mencelli formally as a Missing Persons case without seeming absurd. He decided he couldn't.

Then he felt angry with himself for having given it a moment's thought. It would have been trying to placate Graniela. Powder hit his right hand hard with his left. Smack hands for being naughty.

Sue Swatts noticed Powder hitting himself. She didn't understand, but she didn't ask.

In the course of the afternoon Noble Perkins gave Powder more sheets of paper. They included a short résumé, with little new information, about Leisure Services, the company that owned East Haven Bottling. Also a file on Joseph Miles which listed many convictions and much time in jail, all for frauds and misrepresentations.

Powder also read about the Husk brothers. He'd received their basic records before being summoned to Graniela's office but had not had a chance to look at them.

Mister Jimmy's file, in particular, interested him, being long on descriptive material involving numerous suspicions of criminal activities and associations for Indianapolis's version of a Neiman-Marcus gangster. But the record was short on convictions, with none in the past seventeen years. And Mister Jimmy, it seemed, had never been in jail.

While he was into paper work, Powder asked Perkins for the available information on Gale Heyhurst and The Promised Land.

When later Perkins reported that there was none, Powder even managed to find that fact interesting. And then asked for information on Dolf Manan, the man Sunny Sweet had run away with.

Fleetwood telephoned at four-thirty. "You're going to tell me Jules is sitting there in front of you," she said.

"No, I'm not," Powder said. "I haven't seen him and there's been no call from Tidmarsh."

"Oh."

Fleetwood had had a frustrating afternoon. She'd been unable to get any positive information at all about Jules Mencelli. Lots of "didn't see him," along with a sense that his neighbors did not think very highly of him and were glad of an opportunity to tell someone so.

Nor had anything been turned up on his car.

She had gotten into his apartment. There was no sign of struggle. No note. No absence of clothes. Nothing, in fact, that was in itself suspicious. Except that Mencelli was not there.

She was depressed by her lack of progress.

Just before five, as Howard Haddix returned to the office after an errand, he declared he felt faint and dropped onto one of the chairs provided for people waiting to be seen.

Sue Swatts dashed to his side immediately and then went for a glass of water. Powder and Noble Perkins offered no aid or support. Perkins, arguably, hadn't noticed.

Haddix's infirmity did not prevent his leaving for the weekend on time.

17

Powder went from work to see Robert Sweet.

The boy answered the door only after Powder rang a second time. He was visibly enervated and when Powder got to the living room he found a collection of cans and wrappers clustered around an easy chair facing the television.

"Have you been to school today?" Powder asked.

"Yeah, I went," Sweet said. "But I didn't feel good, so I came home early."

Powder turned the television off and stood in front of it. "What the hell are you watching crummy talk shows for?" he asked. He marched to the chair. He kicked some cans. "You make me angry, kid," he said.

Sweet, roused enough to become uncertain, asked, "Why, Mr. Powder?"

Powder pointed a finger at him. "He's only been gone since Monday. What right have you got to give up on him already?"

"I . . . I don't know."

"*I* haven't given up on him."

"It's just that the man sounded so, kind of, final."

Powder stood. "What man?"

"There was a man come to the house last night. He was asking about my dad."

"What was he asking?"

"Was Dad here? When did I see him last? Did I know where he was?"

"What did he say about your father that sounded final?"

"It was just the way he talked. He wrote stuff down but he

was all cold about it, like he was washing the dishes or something. Like he didn't give a . . ." The boy filled suddenly with emotion. "He talked like Dad was dead and didn't nobody care."

At first Robert Sweet tried not to cry. But he gave in quickly and clung to Powder, who held him for minutes. Powder thought, *Let it out, son, let it out,* but said nothing until Sweet had grown quiet and relaxed his hold.

"What was the man's name?" Powder asked.

"He said something Smith."

"Did he say where he was from? Who he worked for? Why he was asking?"

"He said he was an old friend of Dad's and he'd heard he was gone."

"Didn't say how he heard?"

"No."

"Or what kind of friend?"

"No."

"Did he leave you a telephone number, or an address?"

"No."

"Didn't he say he wanted to know when your dad came back?"

"No."

"I wish you'd called me, Robert."

"I did," the boy said. "After he left. But you wasn't home."

Powder remembered where he'd been, what he'd done, who with. "I was out till late last night."

"I tried a couple times," Robert Sweet said. "But I didn't know if it was all that important." Looking up, "Is it?"

"I just wonder who this man Smith is," Powder said. "And how he came to hear that your dad wasn't around."

"I don't know."

"Have you eaten?" Powder asked.

"Not a meal. But I'm not really hungry. I kind of had bits of stuff."

"I'm hungry," Powder said. "What say you make me some food?"

"Really?"

"I cooked yesterday. It's your turn."

"I can make something." The boy left the room, only to return moments later. "What do you want?"

"You decide."

Sweet frowned but went to the kitchen.

Powder spent several minutes clearing up in the living room. Then he went to the kitchen door and knocked.

"Yeah?"

"Where's the vacuum cleaner?"

After eating, Powder showed Robert Sweet a copy of the individual picture of his father which had been extracted from the wedding photograph.

"That's your dad, isn't it?"

"Yeah," Sweet said quietly. He looked at it for a moment. Without lifting his eyes he said, "Can I keep this?"

"Sure."

Then, "He looks funny."

"Just younger," Powder said.

"And he has a moustache now."

"Does he? What kind?"

"What do you mean?"

"Like droopy or thin and little or what?"

"Oh, it's kinda ordinary. It covers above his lip."

"Is there anything else different about the way he looks now?"

Sweet looked again at the photograph. "I think his hair starts farther back now. Not as much as yours, but some."

"All right."

"Where did you get it, Mr. Powder?"

"It's from when your parents got married."

The boy looked up. "Yeah?"

Powder took out the original wedding pictures and passed them to the child.

"I never saw these. God, Mom looks pretty, doesn't she?"

"Yes," Powder said.

"Hey, and this guy"—he showed Powder—"that's Mr. Smith from last night."

Powder picked out a copy of the individual blowup he'd had made of the heavyweight basketball player. "This man?"

"Yeah! Hey, you knew about him all the time!"

"Yeah," Powder mimicked quietly, self-mockingly.

Before leaving, Powder sat Robert Sweet down in the living room. "You know you're a problem for me, don't you?"

Puzzled frown, "What do you mean?"

"I told you before. I'm supposed to have let official people know that you're on your own here."

"But they'd take me away!"

"Probably, yes. But you are living alone, and you're under age."

"I can do it all right."

"You can, but you shouldn't have to. There's enough being alone that you can't avoid when you get older."

"I like it alone."

"No, you don't. Look, I'm not going to say anything for a day or two yet. Not till next week. But you've got to help me."

"How?"

"You've got to keep the house straight. And you've got to keep your head straight."

"What do you mean?"

"I mean not getting like you were when I came today."

"I won't," Sweet said, perhaps too easily.

"Have you got friends you play with?"

"I guess."

"Well, no sitting around the house looking at the tube all day. Play with your friends. Get out. Do you understand?"

"But—"

"When you go out, leave a note for him. He knows about notes. Tell him where you've gone."

"All right."

"And if he calls, he'll call again."

"Yeah, OK."

"And the Indians are home to Oklahoma this weekend. I'll see if we can't catch one of the games."

Inside his mailbox at home Powder found two things.

One was a note from Agile Johnson. "Come when convenient," it said.

The other was a dead rat.

Powder disposed of the rat, then showered and changed his clothes. As he dressed, he took his revolver from its holster. He emptied the chambers, then cocked and dry-fired the weapon. He loaded it again, and reholstered it. He thought about visiting the firing range.

Before he left the house he put a load of dirty clothes in to wash.

He went to Johnson's.

The fat man had his spoon in a trough of ice cream when Powder entered the stock room. Johnson looked up and nodded acknowledgment of Powder's presence. He said, "Ice cream. My downfall." Without hurrying, he finished the carton. Pulling a yellow cloth napkin from a trouser pocket, he wiped his mouth and hands. He put the napkin away. He offered Powder a drink. "Or coffee, if you prefer. One of the girls will make it."

"Thanks, no," Powder said.

"You got my note?"

"Along with a calling card from my anonymous visitor. A large rodent, deceased."

"I ..." Johnson began, dragging the word out to make it clear it was a metaphorical use of the pronoun, "I saw something being put in. Couldn't tell exactly what, but it was done this afternoon, about three, three-fifteen."

"I see."

"You know, Mr. Powder, there is another matter I have been wanting to talk to you about."

"What's that?"

"There is a boy I am concerned for. Not family!" Johnson held up his hands to emphasize the non-nepotic nature of his interest. "But the child of good area people. The Gorwins. Do you know them?"

Powder thought.

"On Spring, near the corner of Miami."

"Ah, the liquor store robbery on Thirtieth Street."

Gravely, Johnson said, "That's him. Lambert, his name. The boy in trouble, Lambert Gorwin. I've known him from a little child."

"He hit someone, didn't he? With a bat?"

"No one contests what he did."

Powder waited.

"There is some problem with the bail."

"I see."

"It has been set too high. Far too high."

"They must be afraid that he wouldn't come back for the trial," Powder said.

"The boy will face his trial."

"Or that he will commit other crimes."

"I don't think that's likely," Johnson said.

"May I ask why not?"

"He knows he did wrong."

"Has he been in trouble before, Mr. Johnson?"

"Yes. But circumstances are different now."

"How is that?"

"The boy's mother is dying."

Powder considered. "Was the judge told this?"

"No," Johnson said. "Not the kind of thing they wanted to say, you know?"

"I see," Powder said.

"It would be a comfort to her to have him there to talk to."

Powder looked at Johnson, saying nothing but asking him to underwrite the risk.

Johnson said nothing, staring back, accepting it.

"I'll see what I can do."

"That would be much appreciated all around."

Powder nodded.

"And for you, Mr. Powder, I have an address."

"I see. Was it difficult to get?"

"No no, just a matter of following behind."

"Were you seen?"

"No. She just went to your mailbox, pushed the item through, and walked back home."

"*She?*" Powder asked.

Fleetwood balanced on crutches at her door.

Powder nodded slowly. "Showing off again, huh, Sergeant?"

"If you've got it, flaunt it."

"That expression dates you."

"My birth certificate dates me too."

"Do I get invited in, or are you going to wait for me to rot on your doorstep?"

Fleetwood hesitated. "I'm thinking, I'm thinking," she said.

Sitting on her couch, Powder asked, "What do you *feel* is the story on Mencelli?"

"I can't help it. I just don't think he would have disappeared voluntarily without saying anything."

"Because of the way he feels about you?"

"Because of the work," she snapped. "He's got so much invested in it. It's the only thing that's important to him."

"And the only thing that's been making him important," Powder said thoughtfully.

"Yes."

"So therefore he's either driven somewhere and then has been held against his will or someone came to his house and took him and his car from there."

"It sounds farfetched, doesn't it?"

"Yes," Powder said. But he shrugged, to say "So what else is new?" "Have you found anybody who saw him today?"

"No. Nor anyone who remembers his car outside this morning. But, I have to say, no one seems very interested."

Powder frowned. "And still nothing on the car?"

"Nothing. I also checked the hospitals, the usual Missing Persons channels."

Powder nodded.

Fleetwood was silent.

"I trust your instincts, Carollee."

"Thank you."

"What do you want to do?" he asked.

"I want the description put out. I want more people talked to. Somebody *must* have seen him leave."

"I thought you drew a blank on that."

"Not everybody who might have seen him was around this afternoon."

"Prints?"

"I don't know," Fleetwood said. "There's no sign of disturbance at his place. I don't think prints will get us much."

Powder nodded again, without speaking.

"You think I should go back tonight?" Fleetwood asked.

"Yes," he said. "Put the description out as a general call. No one will ask questions at this point. If it's not sorted out soon, we'll go to our detective friends."

"All right," she said.

"You want help?"

She thought. "I think I'll do it myself," she said. "If you don't mind."

"I don't mind. But I mind if you put in a night's work without a meal. You're not going until you've eaten. What you got in the fridge?"

"Your mother would be proud of you," Fleetwood said.

Powder blinked momentarily; the thought of his mother and then of the money from her half-brother passed through his mind. "It's not polite to talk with your mouth full," he said.

"Sure you don't want any? It's good."

"It's not the same when you cook it yourself. You eat. I'll talk."

"All right."

He told her about the recent vandalisms.

She said nothing.

"I worried that it was Ricky," he said. "But Johnson says it was a woman. He doesn't have a name for her, but she was blond and dressed kind of like a hippy."

"Every neighborhood should have an Agile Johnson."

"She lives on Biddle Street."

"Where's that?"

"Off Pine. Maybe half a mile from my place."

Fleetwood was silent for a moment. "Do you have any idea who she is, or what she might have against you?"

"Herself? No."

"But you must be a little bit relieved that it *isn't* Ricky."

Powder thought. "Not yet," he said finally.

He talked to her about Ricky, and the threat to revoke his parole.

There was not much she could say to make him feel better about his son. Not even that she would necessarily have done what he had: initiate the steps that led to his conviction.

"One does what one thinks best," Powder said. "What other standard can you go by?"

She said nothing.

"So maybe I was wrong. Maybe if I had bowed and scraped and said, 'Poor boy, let me wipe your nose for you; let me hold your hand,' maybe then it would have come out better."

He washed the dishes and she dried. He said, "You up to a couple of hypothetical questions?"

She shrugged a nod.

"I've been trying to put myself in the place of a guy who spends his spare time killing cripples."

She looked at him.

"And nuts and dummies and seniles. What gets me is how he manages the mechanics of bumping off so many."

"That's what gets you, is it?"

"We're talking hundreds a year. How the hell would *you* go about killing more than three hundred people this year? And not just any three hundred. You have to stick to your specific categories. And," he said slowly, "*without* drawing police attention to it. That's the real ball breaker."

Fleetwood waited.

"You can't just go out and shoot them. They can't be recognizable as murders, because murders go on the statewide computer and before long, guys investigating one murder would come up with the information on the others. So you are talking three hundred contrived car accidents, or three hundred unexpected heart attacks, or three hundred bolts of lightning. You can't even go out and kidnap them, because they would show up missing." He spread his hands wide, the scope of the problem.

Fleetwood said nothing.

"Of course you don't *have* to knock them off one at a time. But if you do too many in groups, again you've got attention. It's a hell of a problem for someone setting about doing it."

"I suppose it is."

"I mean, first off, how do you *find* all these people? It's a lot of people to identify, year after year. What do you do? Stand outside physio units and follow them home? Or go for mailing lists from crutch companies? It's a real logistical problem. So, my first question: Hypothesize that Mencelli is right after all and you were him. What would be your next question on the computer?"

"You tell me, Powder."

"All right. If I'm him, I'm not worried about better statistical comparisons with other states. What I want is more detail from inside Indiana."

Powder stood back decisively.

He continued, "I want to know where in the state these people have been dying. All in Indianapolis? That would make hiding the numbers harder, but it would simplify the technical problem of actually doing it for the killer."

"So you think there is a killer?" Fleetwood asked.

"How the hell do I know?" Powder boomed. "You and Mencelli seem to think there is. Tidmarsh did for a while. All I'm saying is *if* there is one, you got to look at what he's facing. Think about how he goes about it."

Reflecting on Powder's ambivalence, Fleetwood said nothing.

"Three hundred people, remember. One a day, with Sundays off, all year long. Over seven years. Presidents' birthdays you can have off too." He glared at her. "How do *you* kill somebody every day, so nobody suspects? Answer? With difficulty—that's the answer. The goddamn thing is full of internal contradictions, am I right?"

Fleetwood looked at him.

"To keep from being noticed, the victims *have* to be spread all over the state, *have* to be unrelated, *have* not to be known to the killer. So look at it. Not only are you killing specific kinds of people every day, you're killing strangers, but in such a way that nobody suspects foul play. No forced entries to houses, for instance. I mean, Christ! Carollee, the thing is just impossible! It obviously isn't happening. Too fantastical to contemplate. So my last question that I'm asking you: How the hell can you contemplate it?"

"I don't know," Fleetwood said.

Powder pointed a finger. "I'll tell you how," he said. "By having a lot more than one person doing the killing. That's how."

Fleetwood left to question Mencelli's neighbors. Powder drove around for a while.

He stopped first outside Robert Sweet's house but quickly contented himself that the darkness of the windows visible from the front was a good sign.

Then he drove to Martha Miles's house and spent a longer time sitting outside, studying the front, nearly three-quarters of an hour. But here also he saw nothing that stimulated him to action or fed suspicion. He used the time to mull over what he thought about Martha Miles.

What he decided was that he didn't know.

In the course of his musings he remembered he hadn't told Fleetwood about his attempt to develop a career in television for her. An attempt which had, seemingly, foundered on his neglecting to realize the minimal nature of CCC's current-affairs broadcasting.

"We changed format over a year ago, Lieutenant," Wendy Winslow had told him.

Powder had been furious with Miller, but Miller had shrugged it off. "You specifically asked me to put the idea to them. I did what you asked."

"It's still a good idea," Winslow had said. "I'll think about it and if *we* can't do anything with it, maybe I'll have a word with one or two people I know."

Powder had made quite a fool of himself.

From Miles's house he went to Biddle Street. Here too he sat, watching windows, lights. This time there was movement. Not the signs of a party, exactly, but the street seemed more alive at eleven on a Friday night than either of the others. In the twenty minutes he spent outside, one man came out of the address Powder had been given and three others went in.

In the twentieth minute Powder rubbed his face and drove away.

At Leonardo's he sat at the bar. He ordered scotch and a chaser. He leaned on his elbows for a time, and then turned to look at the other patrons in the club. The room was quietly full. A chanteuse sat at a piano, her lips caressing a microphone. From where he was, Powder couldn't make out the words she was singing. She was backed by a bass player who was pretty too.

Powder turned to the bar. He banged his shot glass.

"Again?" asked the bartender, in his fifties and wearing a red jacket.

"Shall I tell you what I want?" Powder asked.

The man smiled. "You can probably get it here," he said helpfully.

"What I want is one of these guys." Powder took the pictures of Sidney Sweet and "Smith" from his jacket pocket and placed them side by side on the bar.

The man stiffened visibly and looked at Powder, not the pictures. "Never seen them," he said.

"In that case you better get me a drink," Powder said.

The barman returned with another scotch.

Powder took his ID wallet out and spread it, shield up, next to his drink. From a pocket he drew five dollars and gave it to the man. When the change came back, the wallet was gone.

"You want to look at the pictures again or do you want to send for Husk?"

Without speaking, the bartender pivoted and went to the cash register. Beneath it he pressed something.

Through the music Powder heard a bell ring faintly.

A few seconds later Earle Nason was standing by his right shoulder.

"Well, well, well," Powder said. "Long time no see."

"What's the beef, Alan?" Nason asked the barman.

"Guy has a badge and some pictures and he mentioned Mister Jimmy."

"Let's see the pictures," Nason said.

Powder made no move. Nason took them from the bar. He studied them for a moment, then shook his head. "Sorry, don't know them."

"Lead me to Husk," Powder said.

"Is Mister Jimmy expecting you?"

"Probably, but I don't have an appointment."

"Only I'm not sure he's on the premises at the moment."

"The alternative is that I take you downtown for an hour or two, Earle."

"What for?"

"Why don't you ask Husk whether he is on the premises or not, eh?"

"OK." Nason said. "But if it's a payoff you're after, we only take care of the names on the list."

Nason left.

Powder turned immediately to the bar and winked at the barman.

Alan shook his head slowly.

"What's your problem?" Powder asked.

"Usually I can spot a cop right off," the man said. "But you looked normal to me. Maybe I'm losing my touch."

"I'm a terrific guy," Powder said. "Great company. An ice bucket of laughs. But normal?" He shook his head slowly and shared the bartender's wonderment.

The man turned away.

Mister Jimmy Husk had an office suite above the club. The decor reflected a struggle between obvious wealth and sheer ostentation, with ostentation winning on points and showing itself particularly in surpluses of gold glittery trinkets and paintings caked with palette knife-loads of genuine bloodred oil paint.

Husk himself was a pale man with long arms, blue eyes, and thinning black hair combed straight back. He moved easily in his tuxedo and he sported nearly as much shiny trim as a car. The knack was walking without clanking.

He greeted Powder politely. They sat deep in a pair of fur-upholstered chairs made by sewing skins to a collection of gilded metal tubes.

"Would you like Earle to stay, Lieutenant?" Husk asked. "Or would you rather him to leave?"

"Oh stay, stay," Powder said.

"They say you was asking my bartender if he recognized—" Husk stopped abruptly. "Excuse manners," he said. "You care for a drink?"

"Thank you," Powder said. "A little malt whiskey."

Husk rose easily and moved to a leather-topped cabinet. He drew out a bottle. "Anything in it?"

"No."

He passed Powder the drink, and poured a little tomato

juice for himself. "I got some troubles," he said vaguely. Then he carried his glass back to his chair. He gestured to Nason to sit down too.

"Let's see these snaps," Husk said.

Powder passed him the pictures.

Mister Jimmy squinted over the likenesses. He spent longer over Sidney Sweet. "This guy looks a little familiar to me," he said. "I don't got a name for him. Maybe like I've seen him a few times in the club, something like that. I don't recall the other man at all."

He handed them back. "Is there anything else I can do for you?"

"You can tell me why Earle here looked at the pictures and said he didn't know either of the men."

"That so, Earle?"

Nason shrugged. "I was trying to help Alan. The guy was making a nuisance of himself."

"How a nuisance?" Powder asked. "By buying drinks, paying in cash, and asking civil questions?"

"Temper, temper, fellas," Mister Jimmy said, smiling. "You know, my analyst says that half the battle of beating hostility is in spotting situations ahead of time. Take a breath. Cool down. It'll be a lot better that way for us all."

"Far be it for me to feel that our friend Earle was being hostile," Powder said with heavy sarcasm. "But considering that one of these men is Earle's brother-in-law and the other one was at the wedding with Earle, I found his attitude less than completely helpful."

"Who are the guys?" Husk asked Nason.

"The younger one married my wife's sister. I don't know the other guy. Some friend that come to the wedding. Look, Mister Jimmy, I goddamn gave this guy the pictures in the first place. You try to be helpful and all you get is hassle."

Husk looked at Powder and said, "If you know who the guys are, what's all the unnecessary aggro? It's not good for your health, aggro. It really isn't."

Powder startled the two men by rising from his chair. "When I want parboiled psychology, I can get it from a better source than a gangster." He waved a finger. "I'm looking for both the men in the pictures. So I'm asking around. But the extra aggro is necessary because it stinks for Earle to be working for you when he killed your brother."

Nason rose to face Powder, but Husk shrugged, trying to look relaxed. "A friend of a friend asked me to help Earle out. My analyst said that it would be good for me, so I give Earle a chance. Earle turns out to be a good and faithful employee. Forgive and forget."

"Forgive and forget is not how guys like you operate," Powder said. "More like never forget and make sure to hit them when they're down."

"I like to think I've come a long way past that kind of immature attitude," Mister Jimmy said airily.

"How long after Earle came out of the joint did he start for you?"

"Pretty soon after, I think it was. I don't remember exactly."

"It's a nice house Earle and his wife have," Powder said. "Have you ever been there?"

Husk paused before he said, "I don't think so."

"Cost a pretty penny," Powder said. "You must pay your people pretty well."

Husk said nothing.

"I wonder what the date Earle bought the house might be. I wonder if it was before or after he came out of prison. And I wonder how his wife managed while he was away. I'd bet she was petty comfortable during that time. But it should be easy enough to check out."

Mister Jimmy ran a finger along the side of his nose and then drank some tomato juice. Quietly he said, "The theory you put to Earle this morning is that I got him to kill Arnie so I could take over the business operation."

"Yes."

Mister Jimmy set his glass aside and kept his eyes down as he rose. Slowly he lifted his gaze to Powder. "My brother," he said slowly, with feeling. "You're standing in my own office, on my own carpet, with my own malt whiskey in your belly, saying that I hired some plug to kill my own brother." Husk took a pair of deep breaths. "It's a good thing I ain't the hothead I once was, Mr. Lieutenant Shithead Cop. Because in those days I would have had your arms and legs pulled off, slow. You hear me?"

"I hear enough to send me back to the files to see if we got any unsolved armless and legless murders."

Continuing his fight for self-control, Mister Jimmy flexed his shoulder muscles and took deeper breaths. "I never understand cops," he said. "You got no sense of family, you people? Don't you have mothers and brothers and sisters?"

"Tell me something else before I cry myself dry. Despite all the sterling work your analyst has done for you, you still can work up a froth about Arnie. Yet the guy that killed Arnie has got legs to stand on here in your very own place. How come you didn't stuff and mount him, and *then* get the relax religion? I'll tell you what I think. I think Earle *is* a great employee for you. I think he did such a great job first time around and stayed so *stumm* while he was doing time that you've been having him do other great little jobs ever since. I think that the real contribution your analyst has been making for you is to say, Jimmy, don't do it yourself anymore. Get Earle to pull the arms off. OK, James, my lad, that's what I think. Today you get my opinion for free, but if you want more you better phone ahead because my appointment book is pretty full."

Husk's face grew red with rage, but his eyes were closed. "Get the scumbag out of here, Earle," he whispered. "And send Eileen up. Now!"

**20** Powder woke in the night, his mouth dry. He rose and walked to the kitchen and ran a glass of water.

He carried it to the living room and felt for the side table next to his old, comfortable chair. He left the glass on it and went to his front window. He opened the curtain. He stood for a time, looking into the deep waters of darkness, then at the few harbors of light.

As he stood, he ran his fingers around the edge of the boarded pane which awaited replacement glass. Opacity in place of transparency. In his mind's eye an unaccustomed majority of the squares in his field of view were dark, boarded on the high sea of certainty by pirates of doubt.

Suddenly Powder stepped back from the window and closed the curtains with snaps of the wrist. He returned to his chair. He sat. Feeling for his water he found the brochure for the Campaign Against the River Project. He turned on a light. He sipped. He read the leaflet through, absorbing its cares for the poor of Indianapolis and, implicitly, the world; its attack on physical materialism, the heart of what makes America gross.

Powder drank his water. He went back to bed.

At nine thirty he drove to Biddle Street.

There was no bell. Instead he found a heavy, finely wrought iron knocker which seemed out of place on an ordinary dull-green door.

Powder pounded hard. Waited a minute. Pounded again.

He heard a human voice from inside but could not make out what it said.

He pounded again.

The door was opened by a woman in her twenties with a puffy pink face and matching eyes. She had yellow-brown hair pulled to and protruding from the left side of her head, isolating a small lobeless ear on the right. Powder was uncertain whether the style was by accident or design. She wore a long flannel nightgown and she was annoyed to be called to the door.

"So what's so important?"

"I want to talk to you."

"Now?" She spoke exaggeratedly, as if she were about to pitch to the cleanup hitter with two out in the ninth and the bases loaded and Powder had interrupted her on the mound.

"Yes."

She blinked uncomfortably several times. "Do I know you?"

"I don't know you," Powder said.

She shook her head, as if to sort the pieces of the situation into a more intelligible whole. "What the hell is this all about?"

"I want to know why you're giving me a hard time."

"You mean about the parties? Are you a neighbor or something?"

"My name is Leroy Powder."

A wave of visible piece-fitting passed through the woman. She focused and became interested. "No shit!" she said.

"May I come in?"

She frowned, seeming to think deeply about the question. "I don't know," she said. "What do you want?"

"I said what I want."

"I don't know what you're talking about," she decided.

Powder pushed at the door and the woman floated easily back with it. "Yes you do," Powder said. He walked in.

The room he entered was painted black and was strewn with cardboard boxes, pottery ashtrays, paper plates and empty bottles. On the wooden floor, a yellow puddle flecked with green and brown and red looked of suspiciously organic origin, digesting itself in public. Two black couches and a hi-fi completed the furnishings. Three doors led off to other rooms.

"Don't mind me," the woman said sarcastically. "Just barge right in and make yourself comfortable. I'm only the owner of the place."

"Owner?" Powder asked.

"Yeah." Defiant. "Look, what you think you're doing, forcing your way in here? Maybe I better . . ." She stopped.

"Call the police?" Powder asked. "What's your name, young woman?"

"Peggy Zertz. I want you to go, mister. If I want you to go, you ought to go."

"First tell me why you're picking on me, Peggy."

Zertz's face showed thought again, but she was released from the process when a voice called from outside the room. "Peg? You done? Hey, Peg? You sucking somebody's cock out there or what?" The voice was male and it was followed by a Mozartian cascade of giggles.

Thought was replaced by indecision. Zertz turned away from Powder, then turned back. But the agonies were short-lived. A stocky, hairy man in his late twenties and underpants wandered into the room.

"What the hell do *you* want?" Ricky asked.

"A cup of coffee," Powder said. "I prefer decaffeinated, but any will do."

Ricky stood, mute. Anger swelled within him.

But Zertz said easily, "I think we got some coffee in the kitchen. You want to come in there while I look?"

"That would be nice," Powder said. "Thank you."

The pair of them left Ricky and the room.

The kitchen was as orange as the living room was black. Food-soiled crockery and pans and plates and trays covered almost all the surfaces.

"You have a lot of kitchenware," Powder said.

"I see stuff I like in the store and I gotta get it," Zertz said. "It's my one vice."

She looked in several places before she found a jar of instant coffee. "Hey, we have lift-off!" she said.

From an orange wooden chair Powder picked up a bowl partly filled with cereal and put it on top of a piece of garlic bread already on the table. He sat down. "Some little shindig you had last night."

"Tell you the truth," Zertz said as she emptied a pan and filled it with water, "it started Thursday night. Only it kind of dragged on and on. You know, the way parties do. You got a match?" She faced him.

"Sorry."

They both scanned the room. Zertz found a box of matches under a cookie tray and lit a ring on the stove. "It's got a pilot light but I don't like the buildup of carbon dioxide 'cause it gives me headaches, so I had it turned off."

Powder nodded.

"Hey, why are you such a prick to Ricky?" Zertz asked, after putting the pan of water on the stove.

"It's just the way I am," Powder said.

She shrugged. "I suppose we can't help the way we are. I sure can't help what I am," she said. "Not that I would want to. All in all, I think I'm pretty great." She laughed, quick little sounds.

"How long have the two of you been together?" Powder asked.

Zertz faced him with pink eyes wide open in mocking amusement. "Coming on the curious father all of a sudden? Where have you been all his life?"

"I'm not the one who's been difficult to find," Powder said. Then, "His mother will want to know."

"I think he got fed up of his mom. He says she kept nosing into his things."

Powder nodded again.

"He's a big boy now," Zertz said.

Powder continued nodding.

The water in the pan began to spit and she turned to it.

"So why vandalize my house?" Powder asked.

"It wasn't really my idea, but he hates you so much and he's been kind of down lately. It made him laugh, so . . . I like him to have a laugh now and then."

From behind them a roaring angry voice said, "What the hell are you telling him, you stupid bitch? Don't you know better than to open your mouth to a . . . a . . ." Ricky struggled for an exact invective. "A Rule Book like him?"

"I'm just making a cup of coffee, honey," Zertz said. "Do you want some?"

Powder turned to the doorway. "Come on in, son. Sit down. Make yourself at home."

The three of them sat in silence looking into their mugs.

Powder asked, "So, how you doing for money these days?"

"Great," Ricky said sarcastically.

"Frankly," Zertz said, "I think not having money is depressing him. I mean, I have the house and a little allowance from the insurance when my step-folks were killed, but it doesn't give us much for extras. A little hash maybe, but that's about all the joy we run to."

"Stupid bitch," Ricky said.

"Aw, he's all right," Peggy Zertz said. "I don't know what you're 'bitching' me about, Rick. You know I'm a pretty fair judge of character. I know he's a cop, and I know he ignored you as a kid and had you sent up but I get OK resonations."

"Stupid bitch," Ricky said.

"This here is a real fine girl you've found yourself," Powder said.

Despite herself, Zertz smiled with pride.

"Stupid bitch," Ricky said.

"Hey!" Zertz said impulsively. "Lasting relationships are like when the girl resembles the guy's mother. Am I like his mother?"

"Not a lot," Powder said.

"Oh, well. He's too moody for me anyway. I'm quite a cheerful little body."

"And you make a mean cup of instant coffee too."

"Yeah," she said reflectively, perhaps thinking of the great cups of instant coffee in her past.

"So," Powder said, "money's a problem. What say I help out there. A hundred a week? Cash, no paper work. Would that help?"

Ricky raised his eyes in sour, unaccepting disbelief as Peggy Zertz said easily, "Oh that would be nice. Just until he gets on his feet again."

"And you know, he's in trouble with the parole board. They're about to issue an arrest warrant and have him carted away again. What say I put in a word there to take the heat off."

"Good one," Zertz said. "He talks tough about doing time, but he didn't really like it there much."

"He *is* going to have to go see the probation officer. He's missed a lot of meetings."

"He'll go."

"I'll try to fix it so he doesn't have to show for a few days. To kind of work up to it. And then maybe he'll only need to check in every couple of weeks instead of every Thursday."

Zertz nodded her approval.

"You need anything," Powder said, "you give me a call." He took out a card and wrote on the back. "Home phone," he said.

"Great."

Powder stood up. He faced his son, who remained seated. "I just want to say, Richard, that I'm sorry. I know I can't make up for the mistakes I've made in the past, but I'll do what I can to help you from here on in."

"I can't fucking believe what I'm hearing," Ricky Powder said quietly.

"Forgive and forget, that's what I say," Powder said. He

extended a hand to Peggy Zertz. "Real nice to meet you, Miss Zertz."

They shook hands and Powder walked to the front door. Zertz followed him and as he left she said, "Hey, come for a feed sometime, OK?"

"I'll look forward to that," Powder said.

Powder sat in his car for several minutes, eyes closed. He forced himself to think only about his breathing.

His concentration was finally broken by a small girl with a muddy round face who banged on his car door.

"Mister. Mister."

Slowly Powder attended to her.

"Are you dead?"

"No," Powder said.

"You looked dead," she said. "You looked like my grammaw and she was dead."

"Not yet," Powder said.

"Mommy says she's in heaven but she won't tell me where that's at. Daddy says she's someplace else."

"How long has she been gone?"

The little girl looked at a toy watch on her wrist. "I don't know. I can't tell yet. It wasn't yesterday."

"Do you miss your grammaw?"

"Nope. I play with Leon. He lives next to us. His mom hits him but my mom doesn't hit me."

"You're a lucky girl," Powder said.

"Would you like a piece of my candy?" She held up a bag.

"No, thank you. My mother won't let me take candy from strange children."

"My mom says that too," the little girl said. She took a piece of candy and began to unwrap it. "See you," she said, and walked away.

 Powder arrived at The Promised Land just before noon. He knew where he was because a sign told him. The sign was painted in flowing, even letters on a jagged piece of board. The board was nailed to two stakes at the side of a gravel road. There was no fence, no gate, no people. A promised land indeed.

Half a mile up the road Powder found a village of mobile homes and tents. Before one of the tents a huge iron pot hung over a fire. Two men sat beside it on flowery plastic garden chairs. They were cleaning and chopping vegetables. Some distance behind them Powder saw a man and two women jumping rope and laughing in the rising summer heat.

Powder parked next to two other vehicles, a Rabbit and a van. He walked back to the pot.

The two men glanced up momentarily. One said, "Welcome."

"I'm looking for a Gale Heyhurst."

The other man said, "We've only got the one. And that one is over by the stream." He pointed a carrot.

"It's not a stream, John," the first man said. "It's a crick."

"Right. Over by the crick."

"Big Eagle Crick," the first man amplified, helpfully.

Heyhurst sat cross-legged at the edge of the water. Powder approached slowly, thinking the man was meditating, but as he came close he heard the words of what sounded like an old pop song, "Poison Ivy."

For a moment Powder listened and watched the man pound a simple rhythm on the ground.

"Mr. Heyhurst?"

Heyhurst rose directly out of his sitting position, uncurling to face Powder. "The Missing Persons policeman," he said immediately. "Welcome."

"I've come to see the Beehler girl," Powder said.

Heyhurst spread his hands.

"Let me guess," Powder said. "She's out."

"Not at all. We had a talk and decided it would be best for her to stay on Land territory till this business with her parents got resolved. She's on crèche duty."

"Oh," Powder said.

"Not the devious misdirection you expected?"

"No," Powder said. "It's not."

Heyhurst spread his hands again. "We're special people. We're carving out a special place for ourselves in society. Clear thinking. Plain expression. We acknowledge human nature and plan accordingly."

"Oh," Powder said.

"I understand your skepticism," Heyhurst said disarmingly. "I have the same attitude approaching any other religious, political or social group."

He began to walk and led Powder back to the village, where they entered a small trailer. There, a girl read from a book to five rapt children. Heyhurst gestured to Powder to be quiet. They stood and waited as Piggy-Pig Pig survived two more perilous adventures and found his mother.

"Jacquie, this man would like to talk to you," Heyhurst said. "You want to step outside?"

The girl rose. Heyhurst sat, picked up another book, and began Piggy-Pig Pig II. Powder and the girl went out.

"Welcome," the girl said. They stood in front of the trailer.

Powder opened his ID wallet, displaying his badge and photograph. "I am Lieutenant Leroy Powder, Indianapolis Police Department," he said. "Do you have any identification?"

The girl blinked.

"What is your name please, miss?"

"Jacqueline Amanda-Jane Beehler."

"*Do* you have identification?"

"I guess."

"May I see it?"

The girl shrugged and then led Powder past the vegetable men to a large green tent. She unzipped the front door and Powder followed her inside. There were four rooms. The girl went to one where there was a single sleeping bag and a suitcase.

She opened the case and fished around. She withdrew a few pieces of paper, one of which was a driving license. While Powder studied it, she located a book.

"This is as good as any ID," she said.

Powder took the book, a Broad Ripple High School Yearbook. He thumbed through the individual pictures until he found Jacqueline Amanda-Jane Beehler.

"It's me, see?" the girl said, smiling, a pose.

"I see."

He read that she had been secretary of the Debate Club, wanted to become President of the United States, and had the prettiest shoulders in the class.

"Thank you," Powder said. He gave her back the book and the documents and he went outside.

When she joined him he said, "Your parents have reported you as a missing person."

"Dumb clucks," she said.

"They say that they've not been allowed access to you."

"Did they say that I told them to stay away?"

"No. They seem to be afraid you are being kept against your will, or have been brainwashed."

The girl made an exasperated sound. "That's good from them! I've never thought more clearly than since I split from home."

"Are you free to leave here whenever you want to?"

"Of course!" she said disgustedly. "People are so narrow-minded!"

"Do you not understand their concern?"

She wrinkled her nose. "I understand they want me to go to college and I don't want to. I understand that they want me to become a primary-school teacher and I don't want to. I understand that they want me to marry Sandy Cragen and I don't want to. I understand that I am happier here than I have been at home for the last six years."

They began to walk back to the crèche.

"May I ask the basis for that happiness?"

"There's no bullshit here," she said. "No measuring by what neighbors you don't respect think. No bowing and scraping to relatives."

She stopped and faced Powder and said, "No archaic, irrational, self-righteous religious system that says my God is better than yours but means I am better than you. We don't accept that there is anything important in people that survives death. If there is anything timeless about human beings, then we don't accept that what we do in this life has any effect on it."

"What do you do in this life then?"

"We work together. It's all up front."

"What are you working together for?"

She smiled. "Power!" she said. "Power!"

Powder stayed for lunch. He and Gale Heyhurst and Jacqueline Beehler ate sandwiches in the shade of a maple tree.

"I understand," Powder said, "that you plan to take over the world."

"Not the world," Heyhurst said. "Just the country."

"Come on, Gale! You told me the world," Jacqueline Beehler said.

"Well, the country first."

"And the object of taking over the country?"

"To make those in The Promised Land safe from the rest, as healthy as possible and physically comfortable."

"You'll be extending your boundaries, then?"

"Oh, yes," Heyhurst said. "This property is only rented anyway."

"I see," Powder said. "Any special method planned for overthrowing the government?"

Heyhurst stared at him intensely. "We're not revolutionaries or terrorists. We are not going to overthrow the government. We're going in by the back door of the existing political system."

"Which back door is that?"

"The idea is that if we can get together enough people of voting age and move them to a state with a small population, we can take it over."

"Oh," Powder said. "Which state did you have in mind?"

"Nevada," Heyhurst said. "For a while we thought Alaska, but we've settled on Nevada."

"It's warmer in Nevada," Jacqueline Beehler said knowingly.

"Of course," Powder said, raising an eyebrow.

"And there's all that gambling money," she said brightly, "and the prostitution and the divorces!"

"With the right priorities," Heyhurst said, "we can make one hell of a comfortable life."

"How many people will it take?" Powder asked.

"A hundred, maybe a hundred and fifty thousand."

"How many have you got?"

"We're growing fast."

**22**

On his way back to town, Powder stopped at a phone and called Fleetwood's house.

He was a little surprised when she answered.

She was annoyed. "I've been trying to find you. Where the hell have you been?"

He sat on a hard-backed chair. He held her hand.

She sighed tiredly.

Powder wrinkled his face. "No one saw him at all?"

"The only person I haven't interviewed is the woman who lives directly opposite him. She's visiting family or something. Nobody's quite sure and they don't know when she'll be back."

"All right," Powder said decisively. "Take it to the detectives."

Fleetwood snorted. "They'll pass it straight back to us."

"Not when I threaten to take Jules's conclusions to the papers."

She looked at him.

"We'll give it till Monday," he said. "We couldn't get them to cross their legs for anything less than a bomb on the weekend."

"All right," Fleetwood said.

"Meanwhile I want to take you to bed." Powder said.

"What?"

"Physiotherapy. See if you can feel anything."

"I get my tingles, Powder," Fleetwood said sharply. "And don't you diminish them. They mean a lot to me. And things are being done with nerve regeneration too.

I've got more than hopes for myself. I've got plans for myself."

Powder chuckled.

"What's so funny?"

"I'd like to take you to bed," he said. "But you haven't got time."

"I haven't?"

"You've got some questions to ask."

"I do?"

"This woman you haven't seen . . ."

"Yes?"

"Have you confirmed that she *is* with relatives?"

Fleetwood's eyelids opened wider, then narrowed.

"Shit!" she said. She pulled her hand from Powder's and rolled toward the door.

When Powder got to Tidmarsh's house he was told that the acting head of the IPD's computer section was having a bath.

"It's something he does on Saturday afternoons," Mrs. Tidmarsh said. "He spends a couple of hours in there. He looks forward to it. I really don't want to disturb him."

Mrs. Tidmarsh was a small woman, with bright blue eyes and an apparent abundance of energy.

Powder nodded, understandingly. But he said, "I need him," and before Mrs. Tidmarsh could stop him, he walked past her.

He heard singing upstairs and followed the sound to find the bathroom.

Tidmarsh was stretched steamily in an oversized tub. A rack across its sides held bottles of scotch and milk, a large glass, a selection of soaps and brushes, and a stand that held a magazine so it could be read from a nearly submerged position. Tidmarsh's singing voice was so-so.

"Come on," Powder said. "We only have until Monday morning."

Tidmarsh looked up. He saw Powder. He closed his mouth. He closed his eyes.

Mrs. Tidmarsh entered the bathroom after Powder. She began to explain, but her husband said only, "Don't bother to send for the police, Charlene. I'll deal with it."

Doubtfully, Charlene Tidmarsh left the room and closed the door.

Tidmarsh pushed his bath rack away and sat up. He splashed at the water around his legs a bit. "You're always making waves, Powder," he said. "Downtown I find that endearing, because there are so many leaky canoes who think they're battleships down there. But you've come into my house. You've interrupted one of my few private pleasures. When I stop speaking, you have five seconds to start an explanation. It will be spoken in simple English, with no games or riddles. If you fail to satisfy, I'll break one of your bones for the pure enjoyment of hearing a simple, understandable sound come out of your body. And then I'll throw you out."

Powder began immediately. "I'm sorry," he said, "but . . ."

About 4:45, Powder went into the Missing Persons office. He called Robert Sweet. He offered to take the boy to the second game of the Indians day-night double header against Oklahoma.

To Powder's ear Sweet sounded unexpectedly matter-of-fact about the invitation, but they agreed that Powder would pick him up a little after six-thirty.

While he was in the office Powder called the parents of Jacqueline Beehler. With one each on two extension telephones, he explained that he had been to The Promised Land, that he had seen their daughter, that there was no justification for a police involvement.

His report met with deep silence.

Continuing, Powder said that Jacqueline had struck him as entirely in control of her own life and under no pressure to remain with the group if she didn't want to. He thought she clearly wanted to remain. He said that if they wanted his opinion, the group struck him as more open than the well-publicized cultish communities. As far as he could make out, the group's main interests seemed to be secular rather than religious, primarily a plan to get themselves an easy life without having to do much work for it.

"Atheistical bastards," Mr. Beehler intoned.

Mrs. Beehler cried.

Tidmarsh arrived at a quarter past five. Powder walked with him to the computer room, then left him to it.

Powder drove to Fleetwood's house. When he found she wasn't there, he left her a note suggesting that she join Tidmarsh. Then he went home.

Approaching his front door, Powder was momentarily startled when he saw something white in his mailbox.

But it was an envelope that had been hand-delivered and as he took it out Powder chuckled aloud. He entered the house musing on how quickly one developed expectations, anxieties.

The note was from Martha Miles. It asked Powder to call if at all possible.

Powder put the note in his pocket. He went to his kitchen and made a cup of tea.

He reread the note while he drank the tea.

Then Powder called Martha Miles.

"I'm so grateful to hear from you, Leroy," she said.

"What's the problem?"

"You're going to think I'm a dreadful bore and terribly forward, but I wondered if you might be able to come over this evening. I've been feeling low all day long and, well, I'd be grateful for a little company."

Powder blinked. And thought.

"Are you there, Leroy? Hello?"

"Yes, I'm here," he said. "I was just thinking."

"You're going to tell me you can't come, aren't you?" she said quietly.

"I do have something to do tonight."

"Well, a handsome, charming, unattached man . . . I can't seriously expect to walk into your life and take up an important place. I'll be lucky to become one of the many, I suspect."

"I will be finished with what I have to do by the middle of the evening. I could come over later on."

"What time, exactly?" she asked.

"Ten, ten-thirty."

After a moment she said, "That will be fine."

"The exact time depends on whether there are extra innings or not."

"You're so humorous," she stated.

After they had hung up, Powder sat, considering, wondering whether he had really heard moments of ice among the warmth.

He left to pick up Robert Sweet.

The boy was waiting in his Indians cap and showed some of the excitement Powder had felt to be lacking on the telephone.

They arrived at Bush Stadium a few minutes before seven. Powder bought box seats on the third-base line. They got settled just as the first Oklahoma batter came to the plate.

"Hey," Robert Sweet said, "the Indians won the first game. It says so on the scoreboard."

Powder turned to the boy. He expected him to have followed the first game on the radio and certainly to know the result. "Something's happened, hasn't it?" Powder asked.

Sweet looked at him and said, "What do you mean?"

The umpire called a strike.

"I mean something has happened. Tell me what."

The boy's lips tightened.

"Now," Powder instructed.

"I heard from my mom," Robert Sweet said.

"When?" Powder asked.

"She called me this morning."

"Why didn't you tell me?"

Sweet turned away and watched the batter, a stocky left fielder, take a ball.

"I thought maybe you wouldn't, you know . . ." His voice drifted away.

"What?" Powder asked.

"I thought you wouldn't talk to me anymore if you knew my mom was back."

"She's in Indianapolis?"

"She's arriving on Monday," the boy said sadly. "She said she would come to the house. She wants me to take the day off from school."

"What time on Monday?"

"Noon. But she won't come then."

"She won't?"

"She's always late, my mom."

"Oh," Powder said.

They turned as the Oklahoma batter popped up to the second baseman. "I could have done that," Sweet said, and Powder remembered that the boy was a second baseman too. Good glove, no hit.

"I want to talk to your mother," Powder said.

"I don't."

They were silent for a moment. Then Sweet said, "Do you think she'll have that guy with her?"

"Did she say anything about him?"

"Nope."

"Did you ask?"

The boy shook his head.

They watched the next batter line a single to short left field. The man danced around the bag with first-inning energy as the ball came back to the Indians' pitcher. He looked quick.

"Do you think he'll try to steal second?" Powder asked.

"Maybe. But Ignacio's arm is pretty strong."

"You should have brought your glove in case we get a foul ball," Powder said.

"Yeah," the boy said, a little sadly. Then, "Am I going to have to go with her?"

"Do you think she'll want to take you away?"

He shrugged.

"What exactly did she say to you, Robert?"

"She said, 'Hello, Bobby. This is your mother speaking. Do you recognize my voice? Sorry I haven't written. We've been real busy. But I heard that your old man has gone and deserted you. That's a rotten trick, but what do you expect from a guy like that? I'll see you Monday about noon. Stay at home, all right? Bye.' "

Powder smiled. "You've got that down word for word, huh?"

"I can remember stuff like that. It's history I have trouble with."

On a two-ball count Oklahoma played hit and run. The batter swung and missed and the Indians' catcher, Ignacio, threw the runner out at second base. Sweet and Powder whistled approval. On the next pitch the batter fouled out, the play made again by the catcher, who was roundly patted on the back as his teammates cleared the field into the dugout.

"See," Robert Sweet said. "You don't have to be able to hit."

As the Oklahoma pitcher was warming up, Sweet turned to Powder and said abruptly, "I told you some fibs about my dad."

"What sort of fibs?" Powder asked easily.

"We hardly never did things together."

"Oh," Powder said.

"He always left the notes, like I said, if he wasn't going to be in. And I saw him every day, mostly. And he liked the Indians and we talked about them, but he never came to see me play."

"It sounds like you spend quite a lot of time alone, Robert."

The boy shrugged. "I guess. I don't mind though. And even so, he's the only person I got."

Powder nodded slowly.

"Or had. I suppose you're going to tell me he's dead."

"I don't know," Powder said.

"But he might be?"

"I can't promise you he isn't. But that doesn't mean that he is."

The boy was silent for a few moments. Then he said, "I like you talking to me like I'm not stupid."

The Indians' lead-off hitter entered the batter's box.

As Powder parked in front of Martha Miles's house, he saw the light silhouetting her head in a gap between the curtains of her front window. The shape withdrew and the curtains closed as he got out of the car.

Powder took a couple of deep breaths and walked to her porch.

She took a long time to answer the bell, but when she opened the door her face was a picture of smiling gratitude. "Thank you for coming, Leroy. Thank you so much."

She took his hands and drew him in.

After closing the door, she stayed close and smiling and available. But when Powder did not move to kiss or fondle, she turned easily away and led him to her dining room. The table was set for a meal.

"I thought you might be hungry."

"I could eat," Powder said.

"Who won your baseball game?" she asked, slightly teasingly.

"The Indians, four to three," he said.

"I'm sure they did. Let me get you a drink. Scotch?"

"Do you have something soft?"

"You mean like beer or wine?"

"All right, a beer."

"Good. You sit down and make yourself comfortable."
She went to her kitchen.

Powder wandered back to the living room, but did not sit.

Suddenly someone started banging loudly on the front door.

After a moment Martha Miles reappeared from her kitchen. She looked frightened.

"Leroy, what's that?"

"Another late caller, it would seem."

"But I'm not expecting anybody," she said nervously.

The pounding continued.

"You want me to answer it?"

"Do you mind?"

Powder turned to the door and thought for a moment. Then he drew his gun.

Stepping up to the wall next to the door, he turned the knob with his free hand and yanked the door open.

A fist, caught irretrievably in a pounding downward flight, passed through the plane where the door had been. Powder jumped out. "Freeze!" he ordered.

The dark, moustached young man from upstairs stood before him. With hardly a pause he reached forward to try to push the muzzle of the gun away. "What's that about?" he asked.

Powder stepped back and cocked the revolver.

"Hey, hey! Easy, old man!" The young man lifted his hands and leaned back.

"What are you trying to break the door down for?" Powder ordered.

"I was just knocking."

Powder waited.

"I've got a plumbing problem. I came down to get Mrs. Miles to fix it. Is that a crime all of a sudden? And do you mind pointing that thing somewhere else?"

"You come down at eleven at night to get your plumbing fixed?"

"When you got to go, you got to go," the man said. "She *is* my landlady, pop."

"Is that the way you always knock on a door?"

The man waggled his head. "Yeah, pretty much. I had a neglected childhood. I crave attention."

Powder relaxed from the "ready" position. He released the hammer of his weapon and holstered it. He stood back. "Come in, Mr. Painter," he said easily.

Painter came in. He saw Martha Miles. He said, "As I was telling your pistol-packing pal here, I got a problem with the toilet I want sorted out. It's kind of, you know, *urgent.*"

"Couldn't it wait until the morning, Mr. Painter?"

"It's backing up and not flushing right."

Powder looked at the man.

Painter said, "Look, I'm not feeling real well." He rubbed his stomach. "You know?"

Martha Miles said, "Well, I don't know how to fix toilets."

"You're the landlady, aren't you?"

"Yes."

"So it's your responsibility."

"I'll call a plumber on Monday."

Painter looked stricken. "Monday!"

Powder looked at the floor, aware of a silence. He sighed, and volunteered to look at the offending fitting.

Powder was led upstairs to the bathroom. "Do you have any tools?" he asked.

The question seemed to surprise Painter. "Well, I'm not sure. Are you going to need them?"

"Plumbing problem? Bound to."

"Oh."

"Maybe Mrs. Miles has some. Go down and ask her while I have a look."

Painter hesitated.

"Do you want this goddamned thing fixed or not?" Powder thundered.

Painter went downstairs.

Powder had a quick look around the apartment.

Everywhere it was orderly and clean. Both twin beds were immaculately made; magazines in various rooms were neatly stacked; there were no dirty dishes; even the empty beer cans were arranged in a cardboard box.

When Painter returned, Powder was rummaging in the broom closet in the kichen.

"Hey! What are you doing?"

"Looking for a vacuum cleaner."

"What the hell for?"

"I may make a mess. I'll want to clean up after myself."

"Well, I haven't got one."

"How about a dustpan and a broom?"

"Look," Painter said, "I'll do any cleaning up that's required. You just fix the thing, OK? I got you some tools."

Painter held a screwdriver, a claw hammer, a plane and a T-square.

"Is that all you've got? They're no good for plumbing jobs."

"*I* don't have any!" the man said exasperatedly. "These are what Mrs. Miles gave me."

"No pipe wrench?"

"No pipe wrench!"

"How about some big pliers?"

"It's all she gave me."

"Are you sure?"

"I'm sure!"

"Gee, I don't know what I'm going to be able to do without a pipe wrench," Powder said.

"You can at least look at the toilet instead of poking around in my closet," Painter said.

"Yeah, I suppose I can do that," Powder said.

He walked through to the bathroom. Painter followed. Powder turned to him. "I never work with somebody looking over my shoulder," he said.

"Jesus fucking Christ!" Painter said. He left Powder alone.

Powder closed the door and sat on the edge of the bathtub. He thought for a while, then rose and looked through the medicine chest. Everything in it seemed ordinary enough, except for a small bottle of black hair dye. Powder took the bottle out and examined it. About a third gone. He held it, thinking for a few moments. Then he put it back and turned his attention elsewhere: to a pile of towels, to the bathtub and shower, to the houseplants on the window sill.

Finally he turned to the toilet. He took the top off the tank and saw immediately that the plunger was disconnected from the flushing linkage. He bent the wire at the top of the plunger and rehooked it. He replaced the lid on the tank. He dried his hands and then sat on the tub again. He rubbed his face.

He considered going down to his car and bringing up the tool kit he kept in the trunk. Turning the water off. Banging on some pipes.

But then he felt stupid, because he didn't know exactly why he had the inclination to do things like that.

All he knew was that he felt uneasy.

He flushed the toilet and waited for the tank to refill. He flushed it again, gathered the tools and rejoined Painter, who was sitting in the hall outside the door.

Painter all but jumped up as Powder emerged. "Is it all right?"

"Yeah," Powder said. He went to the stairs and descended.

Painter followed him. They entered Martha Miles's living room.

"Leroy, have you fixed it?"

"It was a struggle, but I managed."

"Does that satisfy you, Mr. Painter?"

"Yes," Painter said. "I just came down to thank you both."

"You're welcome," Martha Miles said formally. "Good night."

"Good night, Mrs. Miles," Painter said. "And Mr. . . . ?"

"Smith," Powder said.

"Good night, Mr. Smith. And thank you again."

"Any time," Powder said. "Maybe I'll stop by in a day or two just to make sure it's still functioning correctly."

Painter frowned slightly but, already on his way out, he continued without saying anything.

When the door was closed behind him, Martha Miles said, "I am terribly grateful to you, Leroy. That man gives me the creeps something awful."

"I'm going to go on now, Martha," Powder said.

"But I've made a meal."

"I don't smell cooking. It will keep, won't it?"

"Well, yes. I didn't know exactly when you'd be coming."

"Of course."

"Are you sure you won't stay?"

"I'm sure."

"But it's only . . ." She looked at her watch. "It's only eleven forty-two."

Powder looked at his own watch. "So it is," he said. "Eleven forty-two."

"The night is young," Martha Miles said.

"But I'm not. Suddenly I feel terribly tired."

"Oh. All right."

Powder went to the door.

"Thanks again for coming, Leroy."
Powder nodded and left.

 As he started his car he glanced at Miles's front window. She was watching him through the curtains again.
And why not? he thought.
He drove off, turned the corner and parked.

Slowly he walked from shadow to shadow to a dark position across the street from the house.

He stood there for half an hour. He saw no one enter. No one leave. Nor did the lights in either apartment go out.

All that happened took place in dialogue with himself. In the course of it he reasoned that to have a genuine chance of seeing something interesting, he must be ready to stay outside all through the night.

"Setting aside the question of whether there would be anything interesting to see," he asked himself, "are you prepared to spend the whole night?"

"How can you set aside the question of whether there would be anything to see?"

"All right. What are you expecting to see?"

"I don't know."

"But you're suspicious."

"Yes."

"Why's that?"

"Something felt wrong to me from the day Martha Miles came to the office."

"What?"

"Bottom line?"

"Yeah."

"Her memory of our time together when we were kids has to be a sour one, not a happy one. But she acted like it was roses, roses, roses."

"Mmmmm."

"Bed was a disaster. We had nothing to talk about. I hardly remember how we got together, except that she used me for a while to make some other guy jealous. In the end it was her who broke it off. I had become really sweet on her and that wasn't the way she liked her 'men.' She broke it off with a scene, and she said a lot of unspeakable things. It was ugly. It was memorable. There is no way she could have been half-yearning for me over the years."

"So, she's lying."

"About something. Yes."

"But she was friendly enough the other night."

"That's true. But it didn't fit."

"Seemed a pretty good fit to me."

"And tonight . . ."

"What about tonight?"

"A lot of little things."

"OK."

"I just don't see her hanging around all day being lonely, waiting for me to call."

"Yet . . ."

"It's the things together. Not just alone. Take this Painter guy."

"What about him?"

"One, why wait till eleven to insist on your toilet being fixed, if the landlady has been in the house all day?"

"Mmmm."

"But within a few minutes of me being there, he's at the door."

"Maybe he thought she was out until he heard you come in?"

"Nice try. No evidence for that hypothesis."

"Nor any against it."

"Two, I open the door with a gun in his face and he acts like it happens that way to him every day."

"Some people are better at facing surprises than other people. He comes from a criminal stable. Maybe he's used to guns."

"I *felt* he already knew I was a cop."

"Did he say anything?"

" 'I came down to get Mrs. Miles to fix it. Is that a *crime* all of a sudden?' "

"Anybody could say that."

"He just wasn't surprised enough that I was carrying a gun. And another thing, three, he wasn't surprised when I called him by name."

"If you can't surprise a guy by sticking a thirty-eight up his nose, he isn't going to faint when you know his name. Maybe he assumes you talked to Martha about him."

"True. Some people are arrogant enough to expect people to know who they are."

"Four, why's his apartment so clean?"

"She says he spends a lot of time at home. Maybe he cleans house."

"When he hasn't got a vacuum cleaner?"

"You going to arrest him for not having a vacuum cleaner?"

"She also says she hardly ever sees him. Yet both times I've been there he's materialized."

"But what does that prove?"

"His apartment *felt* specially cleaned up."

"So maybe he's a tidy-minded guy."

"Five, why did Martha make such a production number of the exact time when I left?"

"No, I didn't like that either. But maybe she was just doing what she said, telling you the night was young."

"Yet when I said I wasn't, she just accepted it. Didn't say anything like 'You were young enough the other night, Roy, babe.' "

"First you complain because she's too hot for you. Now because she's too cold?"

"I am noting an inconsistency, especially if she's been so low all day."

"So . . . ? Does all that together mean you're prepared to stand out here all night long?"

"How long has it been now?"

"Nearly half an hour."

"Hmmmm."

"Could be a long, quiet night."

"That's true."

"So, you staying or not?"

"I wonder if there is any way to get somebody else to do it for me."

"What, you mean one of the guys on night patrol?"

"Maybe a word in the right ear."

"But what would you tell them to look for?"

"That's hard. But Jesus, look at the house. Lights on upstairs. Lights on downstairs."

"What's wrong with that?"

"Why are they both staying up?"

"What else should they do?"

"Go to bed."

"Maybe Martha is going through her little black book to find someone who is less prissy about filling lonely time."

"I was hardly prissy the other night."

"No, but as far as you were concerned you were on duty."

"I said I was suspicious from the start."

"But you liked it."

"Yeah, I suppose I have to say I did. It, if not her so much."

"You're a callous bastard, Powder."

"So people keep telling me. Bet my mother wouldn't have thought so, though."

"Your mother is dead."

"Yeah. Well. All right, so why is our friend Painter still up when he claims to be sick?"

"Maybe he's cleaning up after you. He said he would."

"There was nothing to clean. And here's another thing. Six, is it? The plunger being disconnected. I'd swear that it couldn't have just slipped out."

"He pulled it out himself so the toilet wouldn't work, did he?"

"That's what I feel."

"Why?"

"I don't know, damn it. I don't know."

Powder left his shadows and drove to the Police Department. As he walked through the quiet halls, he considered stopping to see how Tidmarsh was getting on. But first he went up the stairs to the Night Cover desk.

Harold Salimbean was on the telephone, sweating, looking frantic. When he hung up, he snapped at an officer across the room to get moving. Then he made another call. Only after that was done did he acknowledge Powder's presence with a nod.

"Something up, Harold?"

"It was looking like being quiet for a Saturday," Salimbean said, "but we've just had a nightclub owner shot in his own club."

Powder suddenly became alert. "A nightclub owner. Not Jimmy Husk?"

Salimbean looked puzzled. "No, a guy called Sorenson."

"What club?"

"The Blue Boot? You know it?"

Powder considered. "No," he said.

"Out Pendleton Pike," Salimbean said. "Look, did you want to see me about something, Lieutenant?"

"Yeah. I wanted you to have the patrols keep an eye on a house where I think there might be something happening."

"What kind of something?"

"I'm not sure."

"Oh," Salimbean said. The immediacy of the shooting overwhelmed any interest in Powder's vague request. "Look, why don't you put the observation call through yourself?" Salimbean said. "You know how. We still run by your book up here." He rose and left.

Powder sat at the desk. He gave the order to the dispatch officer, who passed it on to the appropriate district patrolmen. It was all easily accomplished and made Powder feel rather comfortable. An old slipper, this Night Cover procedure which had for so many years been his life.

He leaned back at the desk.

His nostalgic luxuriation lasted only for a moment. He got up and walked the halls to the Computer Section.

A counter with sliding glass panels opening onto the corridor abutted the section door. Through the glass, far across the room, Powder saw Fleetwood and Tidmarsh. They seemed engrossed in their activities.

Powder wanted to go in. What they were doing was a direct result of suggestions he had made to Tidmarsh and he wanted to know how things were working out.

But somehow even a brief update seemed, at the moment, a self-indulgence.

Powder walked on, went down to his car and drove to Pendleton Pike.

The Pike was not exactly an Indianapolis "strip," but there were a number of clubs dotted along it. They were interspersed with restaurants and several drive-in movies—including the first in Indianapolis, one of only a dozen in the country when it opened in 1940. All in all it was a social part of town.

The Blue Boot was a mile and a quarter closer to town than Leonardo's. It was also far more garish, its ambience beginning on the outside, where a huge neon hostess endlessly beckoned passersby to stop in.

The club was full of police. By flashing his badge and his scowl, Powder was able to pass through the lines to the office area of the club.

There a tall patrolman stood guard by the door of the room in which the murder had taken palce. He gave Powder the basic story: Sorenson had been in his office with one of the club's hostesses when a man burst in and shot him three times; the woman wasn't physically injured, and the man had run out into the hall and to the parking lot by way of an emergency door.

The patrolman said that the man had also wounded two of Sorensen's bodyguards as they tried to prevent his entry into the office. The two men had been taken to the hospital but were not seriously injured. Between them and the hostess there was every chance of a good description. The car had probably also been seen. A lot of people had been in and around the private section of the club. It was the way Sorenson liked things.

While they spoke, Harold Salimbean came out of the room. He stopped when he saw Powder.

"What the hell are you doing here?"

"Only dropped in on my way somewhere else, Harold."

Salimbean frowned.

"I won't interfere, but if you don't mind I'd like to ask a few people some questions."

"Do you know anything about this case?"

"Not really."

"What does 'not really' mean?"

"No, I don't know anything about the case."

Salimbean shook his head impatiently. "I don't have time to screw around," he said. "Stay and listen if you have to, but please, no questions."

"All right."

Salimbean continued on his way.

The tall patrolman studied Powder. He said, "You look like you got things on your mind, Lieutenant."

"Something is eating at me," Powder said. "But whether it's on my mind or somewhere else I couldn't tell you."

"Well, I always say if you feel it inside, you got to follow it up."

Powder looked at the man. "You're right, of course."

"Yup," the patrolman said.

"I think I better have your name," Powder said.

"Dave Hunt."

"Ever think about trying for detective, Dave?"

"Nope," Hunt said. "I always felt that it would likely be more hassle than it was worth."

Powder stayed at The Blue Boot another forty-five minutes. He learned that the killer was in his twenties, dark, with a thick moustache, and about five nine; that the hostess, relatively new at the club, had been arranging an assignation with Sorenson; that the car the killer had escaped in had been abandoned less than a mile away in a shopping-center parking lot.

As the first customers were allowed to leave, Powder left too.

He drove farther out the Pike, to Leonardo's.

Powder had hardly taken a place at the bar when he was tapped on the shoulder. He turned to face Earle Nason.

"Thought we might be seeing you," Nason said.

Powder said, "That's very prescient of you, Mr. Nason." He slipped off his stool.

Nason led the way to Jimmy Husk's office. Mister Jimmy, looking fresh in his tuxedo and jewelry, sat at his desk.

He rose as Powder and Nason entered.

"A drink, Lieutenant?" he asked.

"Not this time," Powder said.

"Not a social call," Husk stated. He sat again and sipped from a tall glass of what appeared to be tomato juice. Powder pulled a straight chair from against the wall and placed it so he sat directly in front of Husk.

"Why did you do it?" Powder asked.

"I've got a dozen witnesses to prove I've been here all night."

"That's almost a confession on its own," Powder said. "When does a guy like you have a dozen witnesses to his whereabouts except when he knows he's going to need them?"

Husk shrugged and then shook his head. "Everybody knows that Billy Sorenson and I were not good buddies, but . . ." He shrugged again.

"How about witnesses to the whereabouts of your in-house hit man here?" Powder asked.

"Now just a—"

"Hush, Earle," Mister Jimmy said. "He's just trying to rile you."

"He's shouldn't say things that mean I—"

"Control, Earle! Control is the key, all right?"

"All right, Mister Jimmy."

Powder said, "To say I 'try' to rile him is like saying I 'try' to get water to run downhill. It's not exactly hard."

"Lieutenant Powder," Husk began, "I wouldn't say I had a blameless past, but I run a straight operation now and for sure I didn't have anything whatever to do with Billy Sorenson's demise tonight."

"But you knew about it," Powder said.

"Bad news travels fast."

"You knew about it before it happened," Powder said.

Husk shook his head. "No."

"All right, you suspected it before it happened."

"I'm no fortune-teller." Husk smiled at Nason.

Powder glared, in silence.

Husk said, "I may have heard rumors that Billy was associated with certain . . . indiscretions, and that those indiscretions maybe were about to catch up with him."

"What indiscretions?"

Husk sipped again. This time he stared at Powder, saying nothing.

Powder stared back.

Husk raised his eyebrows. "Why should I help you?"

"Can you help me?"

"Could be. But what with the stupid accusations you been slinging at me lately . . ." He shook his head. "You know, my analyst says you probably got to be a real mixed-up-guy. I give you *that* amount of help for nothing."

"That amount of help I don't need."

Husk shrugged. "So why should I do anything for you?"

"Why does my suggesting that Earle didn't shoot your brother by accident all those years ago cause trouble for you now?"

"It shouldn't, of course," Husk said coolly. "Specially since it isn't true. But, as it happens, sayings things like that, if they got around, it would be kind of awkward for me just at the moment."

Powder rubbed his face with both hands. "Tell me something," he said. "Are the cops who leaned on me in your pocket or just hanging from your watch fob?"

"It's not like that," Husk said. "I run a straight, classy operation, like I said. But in this business not everybody is as clean—or constructive—as me. Some of your colleagues in the higher ranks, guys I've known for a long time, they see that I am sort of a helpful oasis in the desert."

"You're saying you pass them information in return for protection?"

"That's crude. I don't operate crude. We got a positive civic relationship, that's all."

"Don't they know that you paid Earle to shoot your way into this operation?"

"That is *not* what happened," Mister Jimmy said again, annoyance creeping into his voice for the first time. "It just so happens I got a couple of business deals with old pals of Arnie's coming up that it wouldn't help if my benevolence toward Earle was remembered out loud just now."

"You're offering me a deal," Powder said.

"More or less."

"What can you put up?"

"A lead on Sorenson."

"What else?"

"That seems like quite a lot to me," Mister Jimmy said. "It's not my case."

"All right. How about a little information you probably don't have on Sidney Sweet?"

Despite himself, Powder reacted to the name.

"So," Husk said, "we have an agreement? You keep your stupid suspicions about Earle in the confines of your head."

"And you give me Sweet and Sorenson."

Husk raised his eyebrows. "Not 'give.' Just leads."

"OK," Powder said. "Deal."

Husk nodded.

"Tell me about Sweet," Powder said.

"They're part of the same thing," Husk said. "Did you know that Sidney Sweet testified in Gary for the FBI?"

"What about?"

"What the hell do you think he's going to testify about?"

"Organized criminal activities?"

"And because of him, a lot of guys, former business associates, became relocated to federal correctional facilities. He traded for immunity and a deal to be set up in a new life."

Powder waited.

"The FBI brought him here. Changed his face. Give him a house, some money and a job."

"Is this general knowledge?"

"No. Definitely not."

"Then how do you know?"

Husk shrugged. "Sweet—his real name is Norman Frankling—he likes night life. He used to come here and met Earle's sister-in-law. Sunny. That's her name, isn't it, Earle?"

Sourly Nason said, "Yeah."

"They meet. They do the love-and-marriage bit. At some point he opens up to her. Maybe it was early, to impress her; maybe later. I don't know. She tells her sister. Her sister tells Earle. Earle tells me. I don't want trouble so I make sure none of them tells anybody else. And there it ended."

"So, what happened to Sweet?"

"That I don't know. But," Husk said, pausing to drink from his tomato juice, "as it happens, the son of the man who was in charge in Gary is trying to get back in business. He is a bit of, you know, a head case. But word is he had suddenly been talking revenge for what happened to his father. They like that kind of talk—revenge—in towns like Gary. And if it's spectacular, so much the better. Word is that with one or two repayments for his father behind him, the kid will have the kind of business support that hasn't been available to anyone up there for years."

"So, is Sweet alive or dead?"

Husk shook his head. "I don't know. He either heard what I heard and got out to be on the safe side, or he didn't hear and the son found out from somebody who he was and repaid his debt."

"You wouldn't have warned him or anything civilized like that, I suppose?"

Husk shrugged again. "But the point is, the same kid from Gary owes Billy Sorenson."

"Owes how?"

"Well, after Sweet's testimony broke the thing open, it seemed that the kid's father was about to turn too. Now *he* could have done some real damage, about how the Gary operation was tied in with the other operations all along the lake and in Chicago. So certain parties in Chicago looked around for somebody to take the guy out before he provided that kind of information. Billy was that somebody."

"And is *that* generally known?"

Husk wagged his head slowly from side to side. "I suppose so. Billy liked to be the big shot, especially in front of the ladies. He maybe dropped a lot of hints. Not that it's something people like you could prove."

"Of course."

"Billy Sorenson was a bad kind of guy," Mister Jimmy said reflectively. "On his way to where he was, he did contracts, pushed a bit. All kinds of stuff. Small time, mind you, but with big self-importance. Know what I mean? Not a credit to the nightclub business. A bad kind of guy."

"I'm sure he was."

"So the lead you want is this kid from Gary."

"Whose name is?"

"Painter," Mister Jimmy said. "Henry Painter, Junior."

26

Powder sat in his car outside Leonardo's for several minutes. He was uncertain what he wanted to do.

In the end he drove back to The Blue Boot.

There he sought out Harold Salimbean. When he got Salimbean alone, he passed on what he had been told about Henry Painter's connection to Billy Sorenson.

Harold Salimbean accepted Powder's information with more skepticism than might have been expected. Powder's unusual and repeated presence made Salimbean uncomfortable. But when asked, Powder said only, "I was talking to somebody about something else. This just came up."

Powder gave Salimbean Painter's address, but he said nothing about his own contact with Painter.

Salimbean gave up on his disquiet with Powder. He returned to his job, which was to pursue active leads through the night and prepare the case for a day detective to take over in the morning. To that end he ordered a patrol car to go to the address Powder had given.

Powder left The Blue Boot.

From his car he called to ask whether his observation request on Martha Miles's house had produced anything. It took a while as patrol cars in the area were contacted, but Powder finally learned that at about a quarter to one a man had been seen leaving the premises on foot with a small bag. The patrol car had followed the man as he walked toward town. Because the instruction had been to watch the house, the man had not been stopped and eventually the car drove on. Nothing else had been seen.

Powder drove slowly back to Police Headquarters.

■ ■ ■

He went up to the Computer Section. Through the glass he saw Tidmarsh towering over Fleetwood's wheelchair. They appeared to be laughing, though Powder heard no sound. Powder watched for a minute. Then went back to his car. He drove to Martha Miles's house.

Two patrol cars were parked outside. Not only were the lights on downstairs as well as up, a few neighboring houses showed lights as well. Powder suspected the patrolmen had been none too quiet on their arrival.

It was nearly 3:00 A.M.

As he watched, Powder saw Painter and the two policemen come down from the upstairs apartment. There was no sign of any resistance. Painter was handcuffed, as befitted a murder suspect, but the cuffs were in front of his body—not behind his back—and the three men seemed to be chatting pleasantly. Painter was bundled into a secure back seat and the patrolmen drove away.

Powder sat until the police cars were out of sight.

He got out of his car. He went to Martha Miles's door. He rang the bell.

When there was no quick answer, he rang again, continuously.

From behind the door a voice asked, "Who is it?"

"Police," Powder said.

There was another delay. Powder heard sounds from inside the apartment. He began ringing the bell again.

Martha Miles opened the door.

"Oh! Leroy!" she said. "I didn't realize it was you. I thought it was, you know, police."

She stepped back and let him in. She wore a short black nightie with a light, white dressing gown hanging open. She said, "Why didn't you say it was you?"

Powder said nothing but walked deep into the room and turned around.

Miles closed the door, saying, "You'll never believe what has happened. The police have arrested that Painter man." She spoke easily, unconcernedly.

"I believe it," Powder said.

Turning, Miles smiled slightly and said, "You know it's pretty late if you've decided you aren't so tired after all."

"Oh, I'm tireder than ever," Powder said.

"Well, what then? Hungry?"

He stared at her hard, frowning. "I am fully aware that I have been set up," Powder said.

She smiled, seeming to think it was a light comment she hadn't gotten the point of. When Powder did not return the smile, she said, "What do you mean?"

"I know that your intentions with me are not what you've said they were."

"I never claimed my intentions were honorable, Leroy."

He approached her and waved a finger. "You contrived our reacquaintance. You maneuvered my being here to see Henry Painter tonight while someone he wanted dead was being murdered. You have set me up to be his alibi, presumably while he was having somebody else do his dirty work for him. I don't know what your connection to Henry Painter is, but I'll tell you now: I do not like being used. I will not stand for it. And I will get to the bottom of it. You can save yourself a lot of trouble, a lot of heartache, and maybe a lot of prison time by telling me what is going on, and telling me now."

Martha Miles said stiffly, "That's a very pretty little speech. Excuse me if I don't have the faintest idea what you are talking about."

"I don't believe you."

"You didn't seem so unhappy with our reacquaintance two nights ago."

"I was suspicious from the start. I was seeing how far you would go with whatever little plan you were working up."

"Just how much detail did you put in the report you filed,

Leroy?" Miles, now angry, asked. "Did you tell them what you touched? What you kissed? What you put into me? Did you fake it, Leroy? Because if you did, you were very convincing and the special effects you left behind were tremendously realistic."

"Something is wrong," Powder stated. "And I intend to find out what it is."

"Is it wrong for a woman to feel lonely? Is it wrong for a lonely woman to want to do something about it? Is it wrong for her to respond even when the man she is with is rough and aggressive and indelicate and not very sensitive? I don't see that as being so wrong. But then I'm not a cop. I'm not a person with no feelings except suspicion, no emotions except hate. Is that how all cops are? God! I must be in a desperate condition to expect to get the warmth I need from someone like you." She held her face in her hands. She cried.

Powder stood silent in front of her, breathing deeply himself.

She cried and he stood, for a long time.

Finally she stopped.

"If I am wrong, then I'm sorry," he said, but unapologetically.

Before she screamed at him to go, he was on his way.

Powder's furious confusion about Martha Miles had not subsided by the time he returned to the corridor outside the police computer room.

Looking through the glass panel, he saw only Fleetwood inside. He passed to the door, opened it, and stomped in.

Fleetwood was engrossed in a pile of papers next to a display screen and didn't look up until Powder drew close. "Hi," she said.

"What you got?" Powder asked gruffly.

"We're not done yet."

"I can see you're still working," Powder said, louder and more aggressively than was appropriate. "I didn't think you were playing computer baseball."

"We have made some real progress," Fleetwood said.

"Well, three cheers for that. I'm glad it's been more fruitful than giggle, giggle, giggle all night long."

"What the hell is wrong with you, Powder?" Fleetwood asked sharply, finally realizing that his needless aggression was not going to fade. She drew herself up in her chair. "What business do you have waltzing in here with some kind of sore head when it's *us* that's been doing all the work? How do you have the nerve? Even if you've got a terrible crick in your neck from looking for hemorrhoids, there's no call to take it out on other people."

Powder stood and glared and fumed and glowered and pouted.

But after a silence he said, "You're right. I'll try again."

He left the room and closed the door.

As he turned to reenter it he saw Tidmarsh walking up the hall carrying a wastepaper basket upside down. On it were balanced two cups and some candy bars.

"Hail Powder!" Tidmarsh intoned. "Goest thou that room into? Wouldst open door?"

Powder breathed deeply. He swallowed hard. He opened the door.

Tidmarsh passed by him. "Haha, fair Carollee! Foodstuffings on a plastic salver, upturned empty basket, symbol of life. And see! Imbibables and sweet, oh, sweet comestibles! And too, greet friend Powder, a hale fellow, well met."

Fleetwood did not speak.

Powder, having followed Tidmarsh only as far as the open doorway, said, "I've forgotten what I wanted to talk to you folks about. When you've got something to tell me I'll be in Missing Persons."

Powder sat for a few minutes on one of the foam-filled plastic-upholstered chairs placed for people awaiting attention from one of the Missing Persons officers.

Then he rose and pulled the four chairs away from the wall. He arranged them in a row. He stretched himself out on the "bed."

His great skill: being able to sleep virtually anywhere, anytime.

The first thing he was conscious of was something tracing his lips: the length of one, the other, the first again.

Then he knew it for a fingertip. He puckered to it. The finger passed slowly to other parts of his face.

After a time Powder, eyes still closed, rolled toward the finger and reached out. His hand hit the steel frame of a wheelchair.

"It's a trap I set for gropers," Fleetwood said. "Gotcha, huh!"

"You got me, all right," Powder said.

Fleetwood took the injured hand. She kissed the back of it, then each of the knuckles.

Powder said, "You don't know how good that feels."

Fleetwood continued delivering tiny kisses.

"I'm doing things and I don't know whether they're right or wrong," Powder said.

They both knew it wasn't Powder's usual frame of mind when he did things.

She squeezed his hand.

"If you were a normal woman, I'd make love to you now," Powder said. "I'd *make* you tingle."

"If you were a normal man, I wouldn't be here," Fleetwood said.

■ ■ ■

They went to the canteen. Tidmarsh was waiting for them. He had three cups of machine coffee lined up on a table next to a window. He looked tired.

It was six-fifteen and the building was still quiet.

"Terrific way to spend a Saturday night, Powder," Tidmarsh said.

Powder sat down and rubbed his face. "Have you found out what we want to know?" he asked.

"I think we have spent a fruitful night," Tidmarsh said.

Before going to Tidmarsh in his home, Powder had, compulsively, gone over and over Mencelli's hypothesis, asking himself, "*If* it's true, what has had to be happening?"

Many killers had been his first conclusion.

He'd also arrived at a speculation about who could possibly be in a position to kill so often and so anonymously: doctors.

Then he had turned to trying to understand how a state-wide group could know *where* to find so many disabled targets, senile targets, chronically ill targets.

Even a hundred cooperating medical men couldn't sustain the numbers required from their own patient lists over such a long time. They *had* to get information from outside.

Then Powder had realized that the state computer system contained, among other things, the biggest single pool of medical information in Indiana.

Tidmarsh said, "We followed your suggestion and tapped into the state system Mencelli drew his own data from. Once in, we located the file that tells who has asked for what information and when. That file had to exist for the state to know who to send the bills to for financing the operation of the system."

"Yes," Powder said.

"And, it turns out that a hell of a lot of people use the data pool," Tidmarsh said. "We spent most of our time trying to sort them out. State users, census functions, health department demographical studies. And research projects."

Powder nodded slowly. "And you found someone?"

"We *think* so," Tidmarsh said. "We were looking for someone who had been taking information out of certain specific medical data pools for a number of years. That cut it down quite a lot, because not that many projects last for as long as seven years. Even so, there were still a considerable number to choose from."

"But then," Fleetwood said, "we got our first bit of luck."

"We *think* it was luck," Tidmarsh said. "No proof about any of this."

"What kind of luck?" Powder asked.

" We came across a name," Fleetwood said. "A name we knew."

"A name *she* knew," Tidmarsh corrected. "A name associated with one of the 'research' projects that had drawn the right kind of information for the appropriate length of time. A project for something called Social Concern in Medicine."

"All right," Powder said. "So what's the familiar name?"

"John F. Baldine."

Powder scratched his head. The name was not familiar to him.

Fleetwood gave a faint, snorting chuckle. "The guy who Jules confided in at the state census department."

Powder stared at her. "The one who immediately told his superiors about Jules' extracurricular work and got him fired?"

"That's him," Fleetwood said.

Powder rubbed his face hard. "And why didn't we think about this man before?"

"I don't know," Fleetwood said. "I don't know."

Powder said, "Tell me about him."

"I didn't know much from Jules," Fleetwood said. "Only that he was another loner in the office and the reason they got friendly was that nobody else liked either of them. Jules

also said he was arrogant and patronizing. Jules also said he
is not as smart as he thinks he is."

"Sounds like they made a perfect couple," Powder said.

Fleetwood did not appear to find the remark funny or
perceptive.

Tidmarsh said, "We went into the personnel files on Baldine. He's forty. Born in a town called Smartsburg."

"Near Lebanon?"

"Yeah. Went to Purdue, both as an undergraduate and
then for a Ph.D. Been in the job nine years. Single. We got a
home address."

"And you are convinced that the information he's been
gathering is consistent with what we were looking for?"

"Yes," they both said firmly.

"And what about this Social Concern in Medicine?"

Tidmarsh smiled. "The address is the same as Baldine's."

"Anything about it anywhere else in the data bank?"

"There is no other entry."

Powder pondered. "So, we're saying that if there is someone doing what we think, and if that someone is getting the
necessary information from this data pool, then Baldine is
possible. Nothing stronger than that."

"He did get Jules fired."

"For unauthorized use of computer time and unauthorized entry into various files. Both of which transgressions
Jules committed."

"We are saying he is distinctly possible," Tidmarsh said.
"I think both Carollee and I have what you call a gut feeling
about him."

Powder raised his eyebrows, since Tidmarsh had declined
visceral judgments before. However . . . "OK. I credit that,"
Powder said.

"*If* something is going on. Which brings us to our second
bit of *luck* this evening."

Powder waited.

"Carollee really has a good sense of numbers, you know," Tidmarsh said. "A nice feel for them."

"Oh yes?"

"In order to give her an idea of the kind of work Mencelli did, I showed her how he got into one of the out-of-state data banks."

"And?"

"I pulled some of the numbers I checked before. Then, they matched the numbers Mencelli had given me. But this time they were different."

Powder blinked. "Different?"

"Someone had altered them."

"In the last couple of days?"

"Yes."

"Altered them how?"

"The new numbers," Tidmarsh said, "support Mencelli's hypothesis better than the old ones did."

Powder sighed heavily and rubbed his face. "So Jules is holed up somewhere, rigging his data."

"So it would seem."

"I wash my hands of him," Powder said. "If you can't trust his numbers now, you couldn't trust them before. The whole thing is a con. The guy's crazy."

Fleetwood and Tidmarsh said nothing as Powder absorbed the new information.

Powder said, "You understand, don't you? We'll never know now whether it's happening. Or rather, we'll have to wait seven more years, to get honest data."

"Except," Fleetwood said, "we've got a lead on this guy Baldine."

Powder pounded the tabletop in anger. His own coffee cup tipped over and flooded the table. He ignored it. "So if goddamned Ace was so upset when you told him he couldn't get time on your computer, where's he gone to fake these numbers?"

"That I couldn't tell you, Powder," Tidmarsh said. "But it wouldn't be easy for him."

"Nice goddamned friends you've got," Powder said angrily to Fleetwood.

"At least it means he's alive."

Powder scowled in fury. "So," he asked Tidmarsh, "how do *you* stand on these hypothetical mass murders? Are they happening?"

"If Mencelli's original data was honest, then we're no surer and no more doubtful."

"I *hate* cripples!" Powder said.

Alone in the elevator Powder took Fleetwood's hand. He gazed into her eyes. "Carollee," he said, "I've got a rather personal request to make of you."

She looked at him, surprise evident.

"I would like to catch a couple of hours' sleep at your house. Just till it becomes a more civilized hour and I can get to work."

"At my house? What's wrong with yours?"

"Would you believe," Powder said, "that if I go home I'm afraid the cops will pick me up about a murder they think I'm a material witness for?"

She looked at him as if he were crazy.

"I only said 'house.' "

"You know damn well I only have the one bed."

"We'll just have to make do," he said.

28

Powder woke up and lay thinking for several minutes. Then, decisively, he cleared his throat and turned to kiss her. He watched her watching him as he did it.

"What brings that on?" she asked.

"I'm feeling better. Almost frisky."

She said nothing.

"I'm also hungry. Any chance of a bite to eat?"

She remained motionless, watching.

He shrugged. "I've come off the fence, that's all."

She looked at him. "Do you know what you're doing?"

" 'What,' yes," he said. "But whether I am right or not . . . That I couldn't tell you with conviction."

At ten-thirty, Powder went to Biddle Street and pounded the iron knocker on Peggy Zertz's door.

It was Ricky Powder in his underwear who answered the insistent poundings.

The father pushed past the son, slapping him on the shoulder as he did so. "Hey, kid, how you doing?"

Peggy Zertz lay sprawled on one of the black couches, naked except for a home-rolled cigarette hanging from her lips. The air was hazy and pungent.

"Leeeroy," Zertz said. "Hello, man! Hello, Leeeeeeroy." She made an effort to sit up. She didn't seem to have her heart in it. She failed.

Powder went to her and shook her hand. "Pleased to meet you again, Miss Zertz," he said. "God, are you guys at it absolutely *all* the time?"

A sullen Ricky followed his father into the living room. "What do you want now?"

"Sorry, but I can't stay," Powder said. "Not even for a cup of Peggy's coffee." He grinned manically.

"So what the fuck *do* you want?" Ricky insisted.

"You know," Powder said folksily, "my old mother, your grammaw, gave me some good advice when I was young. She said, 'Son, never trust a head.' But I'm going to ignore that advice. I'm going to trust you guys. I'm going to ask how you guys feel about doing me a favor."

At the second attempt Peggy pushed herself into a more nearly upright position. "Sure, Leeeeroy. Anything you like."

"Don't make an idiot of yourself," Ricky said sourly.

Powder acted oblivious. "You guys did such a good job at my house, when I realized I might be doing a spot of burglary myself and would need some backup, I thought why not go see my buddies Ricky and Peg. Sound them out about it. See if they're willing to help."

Then Powder went back to Fleetwood's.

He rang the bell and when she opened it he said, "I feel like I've been standing outside front doors my whole god-damned life."

She said, "While you're standing there deciding whether to come in, why don't you tell me why I'm getting telephone calls from an inspector called Claude Mountjoy, who wants to know if I know where the hell you are?"

"I told you the cops were looking for me," Powder said.

"I didn't take you seriously."

He rubbed his eyes. "What with everything else that's been happening, I'd kind of forgotten about it myself," he said. "But I'll get it sorted out." He nodded. "I'm going to sort things out today."

"Come on, Powder. Tell me."

■ ■ ■

Later she said, "I am pretty well adjusted to life in this chair. But right now I'm truly depressed not to be more mobile."

At one o'clock Powder was ringing the bell outside another door, this time on the landing of a recently built small apartment building.

When the door opened, Powder saw clearly the surprise on the face of Noble Perkins.

"Nobe, old buddy," Powder said as he walked in. "I'm really glad you're to home."

"Why's that, Lieutenant?"

"What you doing, Nobe?"

"I . . . was doing some . . . work," Perkins said.

Powder saw a television screen in a corner of the room. It was filled with numbers and funny words, a computer program.

"Great," Powder said. "What is it?"

Perkins seemed embarrassed. He said, "A game."

"A game, huh? What kind of game?"

"I don't know whether . . ."

"Look, kid, I promise I won't tell anybody you spend your Sunday afternoons playing computer games."

"Not playing," he said sharply. "I'm writing a game."

"I see, I see. Going to make you rich and famous?"

"I don't care so much about famous," Perkins said.

"OK, so what kind of game?" Powder asked.

"A police game."

"Hey, great! How's it go? You get cases to solve and you see whether you can keep from getting killed long enough to draw your pension?"

"Well . . . there is a danger element, of course, but there is always the chance of promotion."

Powder took a deep breath. "I can't wait to play."

"It's not finished yet. It will take another month and then some debugging, but I hope it will be real good."

"A month, huh?" Powder said. "So you wouldn't miss maybe one afternoon along the way?"

"What do you mean, Lieutenant?"

"I've got something needs doing, Noble, but at the same time a different case is breaking open, so I can't do the work myself. I've come up to ask if you'll help me out."

"Gee, Lieutenant, I guess I'll do whatever I can."

"It means coming into the office and going through all the files that you can lay your electronic hands on. There is some kind of connection between two people, I'm certain of it, but I don't know what it is."

"What people?"

"They're called Painter and Miles. Have you got one of those old-fashioned word processors among all this computer junk? The wooden ones with graphite in the middle. And a piece of paper to write on?"

 At two-thirty Powder drove to the address given on John F. Baldine's personnel file and parked in front of the house next door. The address on Franklin Place was a small, rectangular one-story frame house set in a plot bordered with head-high evergreens. There was a break in the shrubbery where a path led in from the sidewalk.

Powder stood by the opening and studied the front of the property. The house itself was painted a yellowy-white with brown trim. It looked well maintained. There was a small front yard, some grass surrounding a circular flower bed in which a few petunias sought the sun. The two windows to the left of the front door both had screens and both showed curtains drawn open. Everything Powder could see about the house was anonymous and comfortably modest.

He returned to his car and drove on to the end of the block, where he turned the corner and found an alley. He parked again and walked along the alley, passing more than one family outside making the best of a hazily bright afternoon.

There was no activity evident at the back of Baldine's house. Patchy grass covered most of the area. There were a few rambling roses on a trellis at the right of a kitchen door. More evergreens like those at the front of the house bordered the property on all sides. They clearly defined lines between Baldine and his neighbors, although along the alley the shrubs were thinner, as if they hadn't needed to grow so well on the service side of the property.

A rusty trash can stood at the end of a short driveway. The single garage seemed in poor repair. Its wooden door showed signs of rot along the bottom.

Powder stepped up and tried the door, but the lock was sound and he could not tell whether there was a car inside.

Powder returned to the alley and looked again at the back of Baldine's house through a gap in the hedge. What interested him most was an extension to the main building, on the back wall on the side opposite the trellis.

It was an addition to the house that was totally out of keeping, a flat-roofed, brick, windowless tumor about the size of a single garage. It might have been a garage, but no access led to it.

Powder stood by the hedge for a considerable time. Then he suddenly turned and finished his walk of the length of the alley. He continued back to Franklin Place. He passed in front of the house again. Farther down the road he stopped on the sidewalk by a small tree and waited.

At five minutes to three an old black Plymouth turned the corner onto Franklin Place and drove slowly down the street.

Powder bent to tie his shoelaces as the Plymouth drew level with him. The car speeded up and turned at the corner.

A minute later it reentered Franklin Place, having driven around the block. It slowed to a parking place just in front of Baldine's house.

When the car had stopped, Powder walked toward the house and turned into the path that led from the sidewalk.

He mounted the concrete porch before the front door. He stood. He rubbed his face with both hands.

He rang the bell.

Nothing happened.

He rang again.

He waited.

After two minutes he stepped off the porch on the side of the two windows. Cautiously he studied what he could see through each of them: a large living room.

When he had satisfied himself that the room was empty, Powder took a carpet knife from a jacket pocket. He cut the screen from the frame of the window farther from the door.

He took a piece of adhesive vinyl from another jacket pocket. He peeled the paper from the back and covered the window glass at the point nearest the catch. He wrapped the backing paper over his fist and punched the glass out. Carefully he unfastened the catch, opened the window frame and hoisted himself onto the sill and into the house.

Once inside he crouched by one of the curtains and listened.

The house was silent.

Powder waited for three minutes.

He studied the room he was in, finding it sparsely furnished. He had a sense of its not being comfortable to use, to live in. But then he wondered if this feeling was just a reflection of the way his own desire for comfort in life, for soft, deep, warm things, had grown.

He gave his head a little shake as if to put comfort out of mind.

The room was not carpeted. An oval rug covered much of the central floor space but most of the path that Powder wanted to take was wood.

He considered taking his shoes off. But decided against. The noise he would make was most likely to be squeaks from his weight on the floorboards. Shoes wouldn't affect that.

Powder edged away from the wall.

The two doorways leading from the front room were close to each other and he made his way toward them.

One opening led to a hall and the front door and a bathroom.

The other to a dining room and to a push-open door, apparently to the kitchen.

Powder went for the dining room, keeping close to internal walls and moving slowly, step by step.

At the kitchen door he stopped to listen again.

Again he heard nothing.

Powder fitted his fingers in the gap between the door and its frame and pried the door toward him. As it came he got a better grip and opened it carefully so that he could see through the opening without entering the room.

He saw nothing.

He slipped into the kitchen.

There, clean dishes stood in an open, half-filled dishwasher. The refrigerator door hung open. A hand can opener sat at the edge of the work surface by the sink, almost directly in front of a wall-mounted electric can opener. Two roughly opened empty cans of franks and beans lay on the floor.

Through the window over the sink Powder saw the edges of the rambling roses he had seen from the back of the house.

Powder listened.

He heard nothing above the hum of the refrigerator's endless, hopeless battle to cool the room it was standing in.

Powder moved slowly past the kitchen door, toward the wall that the windowless brick grew from.

He came first to a utility room, equipped with a washer and drier and a wall-mounted ironing board.

From this an open doorway led to a short dark corridor. Powder entered the corridor and found a door that had to lead to the entrance to the windowless extension.

Powder stood and listened.

This time he heard what seemed to be a kind of rustling, an irregular tapping. It started and stopped. Its pace varied.

And it certainly came from the brick room.

Powder's heart raced and his breathing quickened. Suddenly his mouth was dry and he almost considered going back to look for a drink, maybe something from the open refrigerator.

He drew his gun.

He put his free hand on the door handle.

He turned the handle slowly and then threw the door open. He jumped into the room and dropped to a crouching position with his gun held up with two hands.

As he pitched forward his knee dropped onto something hard. He glanced down. He saw a human head.

The door he had thrown open bounced off a table and hit him back. He held his gun steady, pointing forward.

He breathed.

The stench of the place was nauseating.

The air was a foggy mixture of excrement and death.

Directly before him Powder saw the tubular back of a wheelchair outlined in front of a large, bright, green computer screen. The light from the screen silhouetted arms on either side of the chair as they struggled to find the wheels, to turn to face the entry noise. A head swung from side to side in the course of the search.

The chair rotated to face Powder only after what seemed a long time. When the occupant did turn around, light from the computer screen illuminated enough of Powder's face for Jules Mencelli to recognize him.

Mencelli screamed with terror.

Powder waited.

The scream did not abate in time. It continued and rose and became self-sustaining. Mencelli screamed and screamed and screamed. The dark shadow of his head began to twitch as the noise continued, as if it were a mechanical thing going haywire. Powder held his position, thinking that the noise could not go on forever.

But it did. Or seemed to.

Finally Powder lifted the aim of his gun to the ceiling. He fired.

As the reverberation of the blast faded away it was clear that Mencelli's noisings had stopped too.

The room was quiet suddenly as a shower of polystyrene fluttered around Mencelli's head.

"Hi, Ace," Powder said, lowering the aim of the revolver back to the man's chest.

Mencelli said nothing. His shoulders shook.

Without taking his eyes off the shaking figure, Powder

took one hand off his weapon and felt for the head at his feet. The skin was flaccid and cold.

"Who's the stiff, Ace?" Powder asked.

When Mencelli again did not respond, Powder rose from his crouching position. He stepped back toward the doorway. Keeping the gun aimed, he used his free hand to feel around the jamb. He found a light switch. He flooded the room with white light.

If anything it made the smell of the place even worse.

In the light Jules Mencelli looked tiny and pitiful.

"Who is the stiff?" Powder asked again. "Baldine?"

"He was doing it," Mencelli said. "He was doing it. I know he was. I know he was."

"What?" Powder asked quietly. "What was he doing?"

Mencelli fell silent again.

"What was he doing?"

"He was doing it," Mencelli said again, brightly. "I can prove it. I'm sure I can."

"How did you get in here, Jules?"

Mencelli was silent for a moment, as if his mind was conducting a search for the right memory, the answer to the question. He said, "I called him and told him I was coming. I told him it was really important. I came to the door. He brought me in." Mencelli giggled. "He thought I was harmless."

The giggle grew into a deeper laugh that momentarily threatened to continue, the way the screaming had. But suddenly it stopped.

"I knew about his equipment room, of course," Mencelli said. "I knew he had what it took to get into the mainframe from home. He used to brag about it to me. He bragged!"

"You came here to use his equipment?"

Mencelli nodded violently. "It never occurred to me before that *he* . . ." His speech trailed away in thought.

Powder watched.

Mencelli said, "Then, things he said. They reminded me of things he said before.."

"What things?" Powder asked.

Mencelli chuckled quietly. "He never thought for a moment that *I* might be a danger to him. He thought he was impervious to lowly considerations like death. Other people might die. Inferior people might. Defective people might. But an exception would be made in his case."

Powder asked slowly, carefully, "Did he *tell* you he was doing it? In so many words?"

Mencelli answered with a shake of the head. "But I knew anyway, you see. I knew. It all fitted into place when I listened to him talking." Mencelli looked up sharply, as if Powder had only just entered the room. "I can prove it," he said. "I'm sure I can." Mencelli's expression became sly. "If you'll just leave me to do it."

"Why did you kill him, Ace?"

Coyly. "Is he dead?"

"How did you kill him, Ace?"

"With this." Mencelli lifted a tiny pistol from his lap.

He pointed it at Powder.

He pulled the trigger.

In a single instant Powder felt a *whoosh* pass his ear and he fired his own gun.

The impact of the bullet's sudden entry into Mencelli's chest rocked his wheelchair onto its back wheels.

 **31**

Ricky Powder appeared by his father's side moments after the exchange of gunshots.

"My God, Dad! Are you all right?"

"Yes and no," Powder said. "No and yes."

"It seemed like you'd been in the house forever, so I decided to go up to the window and listen. Just as I got there I heard these shots!"

"I haven't been hit," Powder said.

Ricky looked around the room. A body on the floor. A body facing them in the wheelchair.

"The last thing I wanted to do was kill him," Powder said with an old man's sigh.

"You *killed* these guys?" Ricky asked, the mortal awfulness of his father's job hitting home for the first time in his life.

"Only that one," Powder said.

"Oh."

Powder holstered his weapon.

Father and son stood for a few moments, not moving, not speaking.

Then Ricky asked, "What is that awful smell?"

"His body's beginning to decay," Powder said, pointing to Baldine. "And that guy sat in front of that computer for two days without leaving it for a minute."

Powder led Ricky to the living room and then sent him out through the window, back to Peggy Zertz. When the black Plymouth pulled away from the front of the house, Powder looked around for a telephone. He found one in the hall and called the police.

■　■　■

A collection of patrol cars was on the scene within fifteen minutes.

The district sergeant asked Powder some questions, curious more than critical about how a police lieutenant appeared to have broken into a house and killed a man.

Powder said it would be better for him to wait to tell his story downtown.

Downtown, Powder was interviewed by a Captain Shaller, who had been called in from a golf game.

Shaller realized quickly that the case would be taken over in the morning by the deputy chief with responsibility for investigations involving police officers, a man named Ferguson. So Shaller did only what he had to with Powder, establishing the basic facts of Powder's entry to the premises and of Jules Mencelli's death. He accepted generalities about the reasons.

Shaller took possession of Powder's badge and weapon, after arranging for the reports from a medical examiner and a Forensic team to go to Ferguson, and he let Powder go home.

Powder left Shaller at ten to six.

Inspector Claude Mountjoy, with his outstanding questions about the nightclub killing, was not standing by, waiting for the Homicide people to finish. Inspectors, even ambitious ones, don't work twenty-four-hour Sundays. So when Powder left the Homicide and Robbery with Violence Department he walked unhindered down the stairs to Missing Persons. One form of home.

Noble Perkins was not in the office, but Powder could see a stack of paper waiting in his IN tray.

Powder walked to his desk. He sat in his chair and leaned back and put his feet up. He rested, and it was nearly twenty minutes before he tipped himself forward to look at the work Perkins had done.

On top was a note, written in pencil in Perkins's fine hand. It said, "You wanted everything I could get today on Martha Miles and Henry Painter, Junior. Here are full arrest records, conviction files, anecdotal files, bank records, military service records, insurance histories, police records of relatives, and known contacts, and pictures. I couldn't swear that this is everything there is—how deep is a hole?—but it's all I can get at the moment. Also," Perkins continued, "I've put the file on Adolpho Manan on the bottom. You asked me for it on Friday."

Powder picked up the pile of paper and hefted it. "Thank you, Nobe, old buddy," he said aloud.

Powder put the documents back on his desk. He thought about all the things he had to do. All the things he had to take care of. Who he had to see, what he had to tell them.

Then he leafed through the information sheet by sheet, trying to absorb essentials.

For fifty minutes he found nothing stimulating. Many words, much information, but the frustrating sense that he just *didn't understand* was unalleviated.

At last, long last, when he came to the skimpy information available about Terry Miles, Martha's son, Powder began to find the missing meaning of events.

He literally sat up when he read Terry's birthdate: two years *after* the death of Martha's husband. And then there was Terry's place of birth: Black Oak, Indiana. The map showed a small town—a suburb?—between Hammond and Gary.

There was no picture of Terry, but the height and weight were about right.

Powder found himself breathing heavily.

He leaned back. He rubbed his eyes slowly. He thought.

He looked again at the details on the arrest record of Henry Painter, Junior.

Then Powder bundled the papers up, put them in a drawer, and left the office.

■ ■ ■

It was about eight when Powder arrived at Biddle Street. There was no noise from within and Powder was uncertain whether Peggy Zertz and Ricky were there. But when he knocked, the door was answered almost immediately.

"We been waiting," Ricky said. He looked pale.

Powder followed him through the living room to the kitchen.

Peggy sat hunched over the table. She looked up and looked relieved.

"What the hell is wrong with you guys?" Powder asked. "I've only come by for a cup of coffee."

Almost gratefully, Peggy Zertz rose and turned to a shelf. With her back to Powder she said, "We've had this most tremendously funny experience."

Powder said nothing.

"Funny strange," Peggy clarified.

"It was like telepathic," Ricky said. "When I was by the window of that house and heard those shots from inside, Peggy had this terrible sensation."

"It was a real shiver kind of thing, that went all up and down my body," Peggy said. "It left me shaking."

"She was too far away to have heard anything," Ricky said.

"It really scared me," Peggy said. "It made me realize how badly I don't want to die yet."

When Charlene Tidmarsh answered the door, she recognized Powder and screwed up her face.

"Don't tell me," Powder said. "He's asleep in the bathtub."

Mrs. Tidmarsh stared at him intently. "Something important has happened, hasn't it? Hasn't it?"

"Yes," Powder said.

"And dangerous?"

Powder blinked. "Not for him."

They stood looking at each other.

She said, "He's in the kitchen playing Monopoly with the children."

Powder followed her and found Tidmarsh, looking gray, and hollower in the face than ever. He was frowning over a small pile of colored currency. He looked up. "Leroy Powder," he said. "You couldn't lend me a hundred thousand bucks, could you?"

"Will you take a check?"

Tidmarsh left his fortunes in the hands of the smallest of his three girls and led Powder to some chairs on a small screened porch at the back of the house.

"Do you want a beer or something?" Tidmarsh asked.

"No. Thanks."

"Not a social call?"

"No," Powder said. He hesitated. "I . . . shot Jules Mencelli this afternoon."

Tidmarsh blinked.

"He's dead. Mencelli killed John F. Baldine two days ago."

"What . . . ?" Tidmarsh began.

Powder held up a hand. "I am seeing Deputy Chief Ferguson in the morning. And, for sure, you'll hear all about it."

"All right," Tidmarsh said.

"What I wanted to tell you tonight was that Baldine had a room full of computer equipment. That's where Mencelli was tampering with the data from."

Tidmarsh asked intently, "Did you find out whether . . . ?"

"I *still* don't know whether all the killing was happening. Or whether it was a statistical kink in Mencelli's mind."

Tidmarsh drew his lips tight.

Powder said, "Tomorrow morning I am going to tell Ferguson everything."

Tidmarsh nodded.

"What's important is that I'm going to tell him that you

must be allowed to go through everything, absolutely everything, that Baldine had there."

"I see," Tidmarsh said.

"If he was doing it, there is bound to be something in that
room that proves it. Links him to the people he worked with.
On a disk or a tape or whatever you people use."

Tidmarsh nodded slowly.

"Ferguson must be made to make time for you to look for
hard evidence. And you have to be ready to look for it. Until
we know for sure, one way or the other. It has to be done.
You know it has to be done."

"I know."

"And you'll do it. No matter what they decide on me."

"I'll do it."

When Powder finally got to Fleetwood's house, she said, "I
thought you were never coming."

"Better late than never, as the bishop said to the show-
girl."

She poured two glasses of scotch.

They sat in silence. Powder drank. He felt drained. Ex-
hausted.

"It's been quite a day," he said. "Ricky called me 'Dad.' "

Although Powder got to sleep easily, he
woke in the dark with a start. His muscles were tense to the point of pain. He
was sweating profusely. He was
gripped by panic.

Fleetwood wiped his forehead with a tissue. "You were
shouting," she said simply.

He didn't answer. He couldn't. He felt swamped with *if onlys, what ifs.*

Many minutes passed before he could say, "The last thing I wanted to do was kill him."

Later his breathing slowed down, and he unwound and fell back into shallow sleep.

Powder was chatting to the deputy chief's secretary when Ferguson came in. He was a tall, muscular man in his late fifties who had moved to Indianapolis from Atlanta in the middle of his career. Ferguson and Powder had had little to do with each other over the years, but both had departmental reputations that allowed respect.

They settled in the deputy chief's office and Powder recounted everything he had done since his first meeting with Jules Mencelli.

Ferguson expressed no approval or disapproval. He listened carefully and took notes. He asked for and received full details of Powder's actions in and around John F. Baldine's house, although Powder said nothing of Ricky and Peggy's presence.

When Powder finished, Ferguson leaned back in his chair and fixed Powder's eyes with his own.

"You don't know Forensic's preliminary findings, do you?" he said.

"No."

"They found a twenty-two slug in the wall behind where you said you were standing. And one of yours each in the ceiling and the deceased, Mencelli. The deceased, Baldine, had three twenty-twos in his chest and one in his stomach. He didn't die immediately, but he was probably unconscious most of the time it took. It wouldn't have been more than an hour or two. He'd been dead for something like forty-eight hours."

Powder nodded.

"So," Ferguson said, "it all confirms what you've told me."

Powder nodded again.

"Let's assume that the final reports all confirm your story."

"They will."

"Where will that leave us?"

"If you just talk to Tidmarsh and then let—"

Ferguson interrupted. "I'll have a talk with Tidmarsh all right, but I don't think—"

Powder raised his voice, interrupting back. "You *must* let Tidmarsh loose with his machines so he can find out, once and for all, whether people are being murdered out there."

"Lieutenant Powder," Ferguson said with ferocity, "I will make my own decisions about how to handle this purported conspiracy to kill, what, three or four hundred people a year?" Ferguson took a short breath. "I won't ignore it, and you may count on that. But you may also count on the fact that *you* will not be involved in whatever happens from here about it."

Powder waited.

Ferguson continued. "You have, on your own responsibility, already conducted a highly questionable investigation. One having nothing to do with your assigned role in this Department and without any reference to or guidance from officers whose full-time job is investigation. It could easily be argued that your involvement led to both deaths."

"There was no—"

Ferguson held up a hand.

Powder stopped.

"Perhaps not, but whatever one feels about that and your entry into Baldine's house, it will be very difficult not to conclude that you have had some very serious lapses of judgment. Along with everything else, I shall have to give serious consideration to what options are available concerning your future around here, Lieutenant."

Powder left Ferguson at twelve-fifteen. Because the deputy chief's office was not attached to the Detective Day Room, Powder was able to slip into the stairwell and leave Headquarters without running into Inspector Mountjoy.

Powder drove to Robert Sweet's house.

The boy opened the door quickly, expectantly. But it was clear that it was not Powder he expected to see on the step.

"Hello, Robert," Powder said.

The boy stood blinking.

"At the ball game you said your mother was coming about noon today, didn't you?"

"I . . . Yeah."

"She's not here yet?"

"No." Robert Sweet shuffled from foot to foot.

"You didn't think I'd forgotten about you, did you?"

"That's OK," the boy said. "You want to come in?"

"I'd like to, but I can't stay now."

"Oh."

"I've got important work to do. But I'd like you to pass a message on to your mother for me. Will you do that?"

"I guess. Yeah."

"Tell her I would like to talk with her. I will try to come back about seven if I can, but otherwise I'll be here as soon as I get my work cleared. Tell her it's important, but if she can't be here at seven she should tell you how I can contact her. Have you got that?"

"Sure."

"Robert," Powder said, "even if she wants you to come with her, I don't think you should go with her today."

"I'm not going anywhere," Robert Sweet said. "What would happen then if my dad came back?"

Powder was silent for a moment. Then he took his wallet

from his jacket pocket and drew out a card. On the back he wrote two telephone numbers. "If, for some reason, you do decide to go with her, try to leave me a note, will you? Saying where you've gone."

"OK."

He handed the boy the card. "But if that turns out not to be possible, then these are the telephone numbers to try when you get a chance."

The boy took the card and studied both sides.

"The work number is on the front," Powder said, and then he realized the boy was close to tears.

Sweet looked up at him. He said, "Should I be scared of something, Mr. Powder?"

"No, of course not, Robert," he said, as convincingly as he could.

From Robert Sweet's house, Powder went to a pay phone.

He called his social worker friend, Adele Buffington. But she was out of the office. He left his name.

Then he telephoned the FBI.

Powder spoke angrily. He insisted on talking to someone, *anyone* who had the knowledge and authority to discuss a man named Norman Frankling they had set up in a new life under the name of Sidney Sweet.

Powder was given an appointment for four-thirty.

Then Powder telephoned the Police Department and asked for Inspector Mountjoy. "I understand that you've been wanting a word with me," he said.

 When Powder entered the Detective Day Room, Inspector Claude Mountjoy was waiting.

Mountjoy was a clean-shaven dark-haired man in his mid-thirties, of medium build, with a cast in one of his bright blue eyes. He carried a clipboard and he rose as Powder approached. "I looked for you, all day yesterday," he said.

"I didn't know."

Mountjoy's lips tightened. "I left messages all over town."

"I didn't get any of them."

"In your box this morning?"

"My sergeant usually clears my box for me. Today I went straight to see Ferguson. I haven't been to the office to see her yet."

"That's Sergeant Fleetwood?"

"Yeah."

"I left a message with her."

"I didn't see her. Sorry."

"I tried to call you at home."

"I was out. I saw my kid and his girl friend this weekend, had a few social engagements ... You know how it goes."

Mountjoy sighed tiredly. "They say you screw her," he said.

"What?"

"That crippled sergeant of yours."

Powder pointed a finger at Mountjoy's nose. "That 'crippled' sergeant is an active, capable police officer. She's your equal or mine in everything but rank, and if you refer to her in a diminishing manner again I'll file a formal complaint."

"I didn't mean anything, Powder."

"If you didn't mean anything, then you shouldn't have said anything."

Mountjoy said, "Let's just get all this business sorted out, OK?"

Powder glared. Mountjoy led him to an interview room.

They sat facing each other across a table. Mountjoy put his clipboard down and rested his hands, palms together, on top of it. "My case is the Billy Sorenson killing."

"The nightclub guy?"

"That's right. Now the Night Cover man, Hal Salimbean—I think you know him, don't you?"

"Sure. I trained him for the job. I spent a lot of years running Night Cover, you know."

"Well, Hal says you were on the scene at The Blue Boot almost as soon as he was. You asked some questions and then you went away. When you came back, you had the name of a possible suspect."

"That's right."

Mountjoy watched Powder for a moment. He said, "We arrested this Painter guy the same night."

"And how does he pan out?"

"He's *it:* description, motive. Except for one thing." Mountjoy stared hard at Powder.

"What's that?" Powder asked.

"He gives you as his alibi."

"Me?" Powder showed surprise.

"Yes, Lieutenant Powder. You. So, you can see why I wanted to talk to you so bad."

"Gee, Inspector, if only I'd known."

Mountjoy studied Powder again, clearly not convinced by his line of stated ignorance.

"What kind of alibi am I supposed to give him?" Powder asked.

"Painter says that you saw him at his apartment late Saturday night. He says you saw him just about exactly at the time Sorenson was shot. About eleven forty-five."

Powder thought.

"The story is that you were visiting his landlady, a woman named Martha Miles. That he came downstairs to complain about his plumbing. That you volunteered to look at it. That you fixed it for him. The Miles woman backs him up." Mountjoy looked at Powder. "How about it, Lieutenant?"

"I was certainly at Martha's about that time on Saturday night."

"Yes?"

"But the only plumbing I was interested in was hers."

Mountjoy had arranged a lineup. Seven men, including the man Powder took for Henry Painter, walked onto the stage. One by one they stepped forward, showed both profiles, spoke. Then they marched off.

The likeness was good. Very, very good.

"Well?" Mountjoy asked.

Powder said, "I have never seen any of those men before in my life."

"You're sure?"

"Yes, I'm sure. Sorry."

"Don't be sorry," Mountjoy said intensely. "It means we're going to nail the bastard."

"Look," Powder said, "I've got an important errand to do on another case. Is it all right if I go?"

Mountjoy looked doubtful. "Yeah, I guess. But be sure and let Communications know where you are. In case we need you again."

"Of course, of course," Powder said. He moved to leave, then stopped.

"What is it?"

"Just a hunch," Powder said, "but since the Miles woman

is lying about Painter being at her house, it might be worth
while looking into her background. Where her son is, who
the father was, that kind of thing."

"Think so?"

"Hey, I got to go. See you again soon." Powder breezed
out.

Powder arrived early at the FBI's of-
fices, in the Federal Office Building
facing Obelisk Square across North
Pennsylvania Street. The building was
notable for having 672 feet of wrap-
around mural, in thirty-five colors, at the bottom. This was
the most colors on a mural of more than five hundred feet at
the base of a building controlled by the executive branch of
the federal government in the Midwest.

Powder was shown into the office of an agent named
Wensel.

They passed the first minute of their acquaintance examining each other's credentials.

Then Wensel called the Police Department. He asked for
Captain Gartland and then asked Gartland if he could
vouch for and identify a Lieutenant Leroy Yount Powder.
After waiting for a full two minutes Wensel seemed to get a
description. Then, his hand over the receiver, Wensel asked
Powder to take off his shoes.

Immediately Powder complied.

Wensel counted Powder's seven toes. That satisfied him.

"You're here to talk about an extremely sensitive matter,
Lieutenant," Wensel said. "We have to be very careful who
we are dealing with. 'Sidney Sweet' is someone who lives his
entire life in a lot of danger."

"I understand that only too well," Powder said forcefully. "What I want is to know where he is."

Wensel looked grave. "We don't know."

"But you know he's missing from home?"

"Yes."

"But you didn't know that until he'd been gone a few days, right?"

Wensel nodded. "That's right."

"Terrific!" Powder said.

Wensel was taken aback by Powder's acerbic tone. "That sort of attitude is not very constructive."

"My information is that 'Sweet' was a target for revenge by someone from Gary. Did you know that?"

"No," Wensel said sharply. "But I'd say you should damn well have warned *us.*"

Powder said, "I only found out after I began investigating his disappearance. At that point I had no idea what his history with you was."

"I'm pleased to hear it's not general knowledge."

"Not with the police," Powder said pointedly. "I learned about it from a local gangster."

The two men were silent for a moment. Wensel repeated, "We do not know where he is. We do understand that he is missing from his house and that he hasn't been to work."

"He hasn't contacted you?"

Wensel shifted in his chair and said, "If he had, and if he didn't want us to pass that information on, I wouldn't be able to say so in any case. We've got to protect these guys. And protect them good."

"Terrific," Powder said. "And do you know that Sweet's son has been alone in his house for a week?"

"No," Wensel said, frowning. "I didn't know that. I thought there was a wife."

"Little Miss Sunny Sweet dived off to sunny Mexico with a new playmate about a year and a half ago. I suppose you guys didn't know that either?"

Solemnly, Wensel said, "No."

"I'm really thrilled you take such good care of guys like Sweet, or rather Norman Frankling."

"Once a man has established his new life and it's running smoothly, he doesn't want us hanging around outside his house day after day any more than we want to do it."

"I suppose you have a standard procedure all worked out, you got so many crooks on the payroll."

Wensel said, "Do you have anything worthwhile to occupy my time with, Lieutenant, or," looking at his watch, "can I get back to some work?"

"Frankling's been set up in his new life for a long time and you don't keep in touch. But your guy 'Smith' went to Frankling's wedding."

"He was invited," Wensel said. "He did well by Frankling, and Frankling was grateful."

Powder dropped his eyes to the floor. He stood up. He looked at Wensel and slowly asked, "Has Norman Frankling talked to you in the last ten days or not?"

Wensel shrugged. He said, "No."

"Do you know what's become of him?"

"No."

"Suppose he *has* been topped. What kind of support do you give his kid?"

Wensel scratched his head. "I'm not quite sure."

"A lot, right? Money for living. Money for any kind of thing he would need. Money for college. Money for baseball gloves. Am I right?"

Wensel tilted his head. "I can check."

"You do that, friend. You look it up in your rule book, because if you don't give him that kind of support, I can guarantee that other prospective informants with families are going to be a hell of a lot less likely to step forward with their mouths open . . ."

Wensel frowned.

Powder lifted a finger, glowered. ". . . when they read

about what hasn't happened for the Sweet kid in all the papers."

35

When Sunny Sweet, Robert's mother, answered the door, Powder was shocked. The radiance, the prettiness, even the smallness of her wedding photographs were all gone. Only the blond hair remained and that appeared plasticky.

"Don't just stand there like a dummy, mister. What you want?"

"Mrs. Sweet?"

She sighed long and hard. "Yeah, I guess. You're the cop, huh?"

Powder identified himself.

She drew her shoulders back. "I want a little talk with you. Why have you been interfering in Bobby's life, huh? Why the hell didn't you tell *me* when his old man split? Why did you leave him on his own here? What kind of cop are you, old fella? Take the kid to ball games. Give him food. Maybe I should have reported you soon as he told me about you. Pick on a lot of lonely kids, do you? Only way you can get your kicks now? Huh? Hey? I got it right?" She snorted.

Slowly and clearly Powder said, "I want to inform you of your rights. You have the right to remain silent. If you choose—"

The woman's attitude changed like a switch of channels. "Hey, man, don't do that. I wasn't serious."

"I have some questions to ask you, Mrs. Sweet."

She twitched her head sulkily. "What questions?"

Powder stood, silent.

"You wanna come in, I guess." The woman stepped back.

Powder entered the house.

In the front hall he asked, "Is your Dolf here?"

"What do you know about Dolf?"

"Is he here?"

"No, he's not here."

"Are you still with him?"

"Course I'm still with him!"

"So he came back from Mexico with you, but he is not in the house at the present time?"

"Yeah, that's right."

"Is Robert here?"

"Yeah. He's in his room."

Powder looked at her suspiciously.

"He's reading some goddamn baseball magazine I bought him. I told him I wanted to see you alone. All right?"

"We'll talk in the kitchen," Powder said.

"Oh will we?"

Powder walked to the kitchen. Sunny Sweet followed.

Powder took out his notebook. He dropped it on the kitchen table. It landed with a bang. He sat down. He flipped the notebook open. He headed a page with the date and address and her name.

Sunny Sweet watched him at first, then tried to peer at what he was writing.

Without looking up, Powder said, "Sit down, Mrs. Sweet."

Slowly, she took a chair across the table from him.

"So," Powder said, "when did you and Manan get back to Indianapolis?"

Slowly she said, "Yesterday."

"When did you leave Mexico?"

"Couple of days before that."

"Show me your border papers," Powder said.

"What?"

"Your passport, visa, whatever documents you stayed in Mexico on. I want to see them."

"We didn't—"

"Yes you did."

"We got here, Indianapolis, yesterday. Was that what you was asking?"

Powder waited.

"We left Mexico a couple of weeks ago."

"When?" Sharply.

"A couple of months ago."

"Why did you leave Mexico?"

"Well, it's nice there and all that but—"

Powder lifted his eyes to meet the woman's. "Do not waste my time, Mrs. Sweet," he said with all the considerable menace at his command.

"Yeah, all right. Just don't nag me, all right? You remind me of my goddamn mother, you do. No wonder you cook frozen pizza for my kid. You're just like a goddamn old woman!" She snorted a laugh.

Powder waited.

"We left 'cause Dolf got into a little trouble."

"As in police trouble?"

Mimicking nasally, "As in police trouble." Then, "What do you think? I got him pregnant?"

"Was he arrested, or did you beat it by getting over the border?"

"If he'd been arrested we wouldn't goddamn be here, would we? You know what it's like down there, do you, old-lady cop? It's like a big pile of dogshit to get arrested down there. We sure as hell did skip it over the border."

"Drug trouble?"

Sunny Sweet said nothing.

"I asked you whether Dolf got into drug trouble, Mrs. Sweet," Powder said with force.

"Yeah, drug trouble," she said reluctantly. After a moment she added, "It was all a setup. None of it was true."

"I've read his police record," Powder said.

"Yeah, well, he went straight when we left," she said defiantly.

"When you left Mexico, where did you go?"

"Here and there."

"Where and where?"

"Southern Cal. We went to Denver for a few days. Last week we spent in St. Louis."

"Working your way back to Indianapolis?"

"It wasn't quite, like, planned that way, but we don't know nobody nowhere else."

"Short of money?"

"Of course we were goddamn short of money! We had money, we could go live anywhere."

"So," Powder said slowly and clearly, "because you were short of money, you sold the information about Sidney Sweet's real identity to the Gary people."

Sunny Sweet froze as if snapped by a camera. She stayed that way, not breathing or blinking or, seemingly, alive for several seconds.

When she took a breath it was not immediately followed by another. They came one at a time, jerkily.

"Have you had your money yet?" Powder asked.

She breathed hard. "I ain't saying nothing."

"Or is Dolf out trying to get that sorted out now?" Powder nodded to encourage her.

Sullenly she nodded back.

"Did you know," Powder asked carefully, "that Henry Painter has been arrested?"

The news was another shock. Eventually she asked, pathetically, "Has he?"

"So you haven't had your money yet?"

She shook her head.

"You passed the information by telephone, maybe thought it was best not to be around when it actually happened?"

To this she nodded slowly.

"What's Dolf going to do when he finds out you aren't going to get the money?"

"I don't know," she said weakly.

"Leave you?"

She didn't shake her head. She looked at Powder. She said, "Painter's in jail?"

"Sure is. And he's going to be there for a long, long time."

"You couldn't, like, arrange for Dolf to see him maybe?"

Powder said nothing.

"Hey, could you do that for me, please? I'd be real grateful," she said, the glimmer of a plan enabling her to muster a semblance of flirtatiousness.

Powder said nothing.

"I can be good," she said. "I really can. I'd be grateful to you. I'd be grateful to you now if you wanted."

Powder watched the woman.

"Or later. Whenever you like. Or . . ." she said, thinking, "or maybe we could find something else. Hey, you got a soft spot for Bobby, don't you? He said you was a good friend to him when he was alone. You want me to fix it so you get a little time alone with him? That suit you better? A little time alone with Bobby? Hey, me, I don't mind. It's a big world. I understand. It takes all kinds."

Powder waited, again, at Fleetwood's front door.

For a change, when she opened it neither of them spoke. She made way and he came in.

He sat in an armchair and she rolled up next to him. She took his hand. She said, "You look terrible, Powder."

"That's funny," he said. "You look pretty good to me."

"How was Ferguson?"

"Businesslike. He understood what I was trying to do. He'll take some time to think about whether he's sympathetic to it."

"And then?"

"I hope he'll make it easy and put Tidmarsh to work proving whether Ace was right that something was happening or not."

"And if he doesn't?"

"Tidmarsh is committed to doing it anyway."

"I see."

"For sure it's out of my hands now. Ferguson's other problem will be to decide what to do with me."

Fleetwood watched as Powder smiled at her. "Most likely is that they will overlook my indiscretions if I agree to retire."

"Oh."

"I took a lot upon myself that our friends in the higher ranks do not generally incline to look favorably on."

"You got a lot of results."

"That's true," Powder said. He shrugged. "I would think that I could probably fight it. Kind of depends whether I'm feeling combative."

"When have you not?"

"But maybe I *should* retire, for myself. Look at it. I spend years as a team cop, a book cop, and then suddenly I'm out there trying to do it alone. That's got to be a symptom of something, doesn't it?"

"You going to start crying for yourself, or what?"

"All I'm saying is there's no need to rush a decision."

"Maybe Ferguson'll be all right," Fleetwood said.

"There is always that possibility."

Fleetwood looked at him. "Retire, huh? Sit around and watch the soap operas all day long?"

Powder nodded vigorously. "I got a lot of catching up to do on the stories."

Fleetwood sniffed.

"Something else crossed my mind to ask you, Sergeant."

"Oh yeah? What's that?"

"You ever consider taking on a child?"

"A what?"

"I didn't say *baby*."

She waited.

"I was thinking more like a twelve-year-old kid. Already house-trained. Good glove. What you think? Good idea?"

"No," she said softly.

"No, I suppose it isn't."

"Robert Sweet?"

"It's just I met his mother today. But it's all right. Afterwards I took him to my social-worker contact and they're going to look after him. And I'm also making sure that the FBI gives him plenty of money."

Fleetwood looked at Powder sadly.

"Oh, come on," Powder said. "There are worse things than a kid having plenty of money."

"You've had a busy day, Leroy."

"I like to keep active," Powder said.

"You saw Mountjoy too, didn't you?"

"Sure did, ma'am. You name 'em, I've seen 'em."

"And?"

"I broke down the perfect alibi."

"Oh, yes?"

"You remember that woman who came in the other day? Martha Miles?"

Fleetwood's face showed clearly that she remembered the name, the woman and the circumstances.

"Well, she's had a rough time, the poor dear."

Fleetwood was uncertain what Powder was getting at.

"After her husband died—and maybe before—I *think* she was the 'other woman' for a small-scale gangland boss in

Gary named Henry Painter, Senior. I also think she bore
him a son, only when the kid was six, Painter was murdered
to keep him from talking to the FBI. It was a contract job,
completed by Billy Sorenson. Bad luck on Martha."

"You 'think' . . . ?"

"What I am sure of is that there is a strong physical resem-
blance between Martha's son—Terry—and Painter's other
son, Henry Junior. Junior was born to Painter's wife a couple of years before Terry."

Powder paused. Fleetwood said nothing, but was atten-
tive.

"Junior—he's twenty-two—seems to have decided recently that it was time to settle the old family scores and that
meant killing Billy Sorenson. Now it was always possible
that Junior could do it and get clean away, but in case he
didn't, Junior decided it would be a smart move to set himself up with a real good alibi."

"Involving . . . Terry?"

"With the same kind of moustache, hair colored to match
exactly and no chance to look at them together, you couldn't
say which was which. The idea was to arrange things so that
someone reliable was seeing Martha's kid while Painter was
doing his killing. The reliable person would be told he was
seeing Painter, so he could give an alibi. And who is more
reliable as a witness than a cop?"

"They set you up," Fleetwood said slowly. "The whole
thing was to set you up."

"That's right. Martha becomes reacquainted. Makes sure
I am there. Makes sure I know what time it is. Makes sure I
see the imitation Painter while the real Painter is elsewhere,
doing his business."

"I see," Fleetwood said quietly.

"Now on an ordinary day, I would just have helped
Mountjoy arrest the bunch of them and sort it out."

"But today?"

"I had other things to do. So I denied having seen Painter.

Hence he has no alibi and will go down for his killing." Powder spread his hands innocently. "After all, I *didn't* see Painter at Miles's house, did I? Even if I didn't know it at the time."

"Martha's not going to be very happy with you, Leroy."

"Good."

"Tough guy, huh?"

"More important, there are people who aren't going to be very happy with her, or her son. People likely to make their feelings known." He hesitated, and shrugged. "Anyway, I put Mountjoy on the right track. Probably he'll get there even if I don't say anything else."

"You're high as a kite with all this," Fleetwood said.

"It certainly makes a change from trying and trying but getting nowhere."

She nodded.

"I think Painter Junior is responsible for Sidney Sweet's disappearance too," Powder said. "All part of the same business."

"So Robert's father is dead?"

"I'm sure, gut feeling, that he is. But I'll check it out. Maybe I'll muscle Mister Jimmy into finding out for me. When I get a chance."

"Is there anything you haven't done today?"

"I can think of four things," Powder said.

"Yes?"

He smiled. "The second is to ask you how Howard Haddix is doing on that case where he's looking for the father of a girl who's getting married. The father that left home eighteen-odd years ago. Did Howard find the guy yet?"

"Not as far as I know."

"Howard was well enough to come to work today?"

"Yeah."

"He would have told you if he did anything good."

"I guess so."

"Right. So I've decided to send the girl a present, from her absent father." Powder held up his hands to quell a response. "I feel like it, so I'm going to do it. It's just I haven't done it yet today. So the third thing was to talk to this lawyer guy about the money I got coming."

"What you going to say?"

"That he should stick the money away. I'll think about what to do with it later."

"And the fourth thing?"

"I haven't had anything to eat tonight."

"Ah," Fleetwood said.

"Now do tell me if I'm imposing, Carollee, but I thought, if it was OK with you, I would invite my boy, Ricky, and his girl friend to eat with us tonight."

Fleetwood blinked a few times as she took this in.

"I thought I'd call them now. I thought they could bring in the biggest goddamn takeout meal any of us has ever seen. My treat. To celebrate my inheritance. Maybe even my retirement. That all right?"

Fleetwood shrugged. "If it's what you want."

"I'll call them, tell them to get here in, say, an hour, an hour and a half."

Fleetwood looked momentarily puzzled.

"Why so long?" Powder asked rhetorically. "Well, about that first thing I haven't done today . . ."

"Ricky," Fleetwood said, "do finish it off if you're inclined to. I think everyone else is done."

"Oh. Right. Great," Ricky said.

Powder smiled at Peggy Zertz. "From a child he was never happier than when he had something in his mouth."

"Aw, for Christ's sake, Father!"

Powder said, "Hey, couple of days ago I came across some people I thought you guys might be interested in. Got themselves a nice little cult."

"A cult?" Ricky asked with distaste through his food.

"No, no. Don't be like that. These people got a good thing

going. Going to take over the country and end up rich without having to work for it. It's the American dream."

"Ricky's not afraid of work," Peggy Zertz said. "Are you, hon?"

"Don't be stupid."

"He's not. Honest. It's just a matter of getting into the right kind of situation. Something he can live with and grow with."

Powder nodded, but did not speak.

"I mean," Peggy said, "we were talking on the way here. We were saying what with you maybe having to retire, maybe we wouldn't take that money you said you were going to start giving him. We *can* get along."

"That's real considerate," Powder said. "But I think I'll be able to help you out, at least for a while."

"Wouldn't want it forever," Ricky said.

Powder beamed. "We'll all just take things one day at a time then, shall we?"

"Yeah, I guess," Ricky said.

Powder exchanged glances with Fleetwood. He said, "We'll see what fate brings us. Meanwhile, lick your plates, drink up! Peggy, can I light that ciggy for you? Come on, guys, it's kind of like a party, right?"